About th

Bruce has a varied background, starting his working-life as an engineer. He then went on to work as an Oncology Nurse at the Royal Marsden Hospital in London. For the last twenty-four years, he has worked in the Oncology Pharmaceutical industry, including running his own consultancy company for the last ten years.

He has always had a passion for illustration and has recently begun writing and illustrating books. He lives with his wife in the Southeast of England and has two grown-up children.

'Seeing' is his second published book for children, which is a sequel to his first book 'Drifting.'

Dedication to Solo and Storm

Writing and illustrating 'Seeing,' has been a labour of love, which I dedicate to our loyal feline companions, Solo and Storm, in return for all the entertainment they have given us over the course of their lives.

Whilst being very sad to see their love-hate relationship and Storm's intolerance of her disadvantaged mother Solo, I was inspired to examine my own attitudes towards other people.

During my writing, I have come to realise that many of us can experience difficulty in fully appreciating one another's challenges that we often encounter during our lives.

I hope, like me, you have enjoyed the experience of 'Seeing' and that Solo and Storm's story has helped you to see things more clearly.

From all of us who are touched by 'Seeing'; thank you, Solo and Storm.

~~~ Solo and Storm ~~~

Bruce Gilligan

SEEING

AUSTIN MACAULEY PUBLISHERS™
LONDON • CAMBRIDGE • NEW YORK • SHARJAH

Copyright © Bruce Gilligan (2019)

The right of Bruce Gilligan to be identified as author of this work has been asserted by him in accordance with section 77 and 78 of the Copyright, Designs and Patents Act 1988.

All rights reserved. No part of this publication may be reproduced, stored in a retrieval system, or transmitted in any form or by any means, electronic, mechanical, photocopying, recording, or otherwise, without the prior permission of the publishers.

Any person who commits any unauthorised act in relation to this publication may be liable to criminal prosecution and civil claims for damages.

A CIP catalogue record for this title is available from the British Library.

ISBN 9781528919432 (Paperback)
ISBN 9781528919449 (Hardback)
ISBN 9781528919456 (Kindle e-Book)
ISBN 9781528962698 (Epub e-Book)
www.austinmacauley.com

First Published (2019)
Austin Macauley Publishers Ltd
25 Canada Square
Canary Wharf
London
E14 5LQ

All the characters in this book are entirely fictitious and any resemblance to anyone living or dead is purely coincidental…but extremely amusing nonetheless!

Acknowledgements

A special thank you to my long-suffering partner, Juliette. My 'Seeing' would never have been accomplished without your continued encouragement and support. Thank you.

For parents with challenging children, or children with challenging parents.

So, for most of us then!

"Seeing is more than simply having the power of sight; it also requires the ability to understand and recognise the true value of life."

(Bruce Gilligan 2019)

Table of Contents

Foreword	10
Chapter 1 Leap of Faith!	11
Chapter 2 Moving Home!	22
Chapter 3 Go with the Flow!	36
Chaper 4 London's Underground!	51
Chapter 5 Beggars Belief!	64
Chapter 6 Rich Pickings!	79
Chapter 7 Mind the Gap!	92
Chapter 8 Tunnel Vision	106
Chapter 9 Lost and Found!	120
Chapter 10 The Purrfect Mother!	132

Foreword

'Seeing' is a sequel to Bruce's first children's book 'Drifting' and, like its predecessor, it should appeal to both children and parents alike. The story examines the sensitive and sometimes challenging topics of single parenthood and disability.

In a humorous but sensitive manner with the aid of illustrations, 'Seeing' follows the challenges a feline mother and her long-suffering daughter face in search of their missing home. As they encounter one obstacle after another, our intrepid duo are forced to address their dysfunctional mother and daughter relationship. During their adventure they learn to appreciate one another's true value and realise no bond is stronger than a mother's love for their children.

Join them on their journey of discovery and hold tight while you are taken on a roller coaster ride of emotion and adventure. Perhaps it will challenge you to examine your own limitations and values, whilst realising none of us are perfect. I hope you regard 'Seeing' as valuable to you!

Bruce Gilligan 2019

Chapter 1
Leap of Faith!

It was later than usual, by the time Solo had fumbled her way through the house and found her bed for the night. The damp air caused by the heavy rain over the past few days was affecting her ability to sniff her way in search of a suitable resting place. Eventually, she had decided on one particular cushion that particular night because she always felt safe there. It was out of reach of the family dog, Bracken's overly enthusiastic tail-wagging, which usually resulted in at least a few inappropriate slaps across her face; typically, just when she was dropping off to sleep. As Solo circled round and round the cushion in her habitual fashion, feeling for the most comfortable position, she began to recollect just how quiet Bracken had been lately. *He's been in the cellar with our owner Grant, a lot lately*, she reminded herself, *making an awful racket; hammering and banging all day long. Which come to think of it,* she considered, *wasn't being quiet at all.*

"Are you going to lie down or what?" Storm spat out, which startled Solo. "Only you've been spinning round and round on that cushion about a hundred times now, and some of us are trying to rest." Solo hadn't noticed her daughter had already laid claim to the same safe spot.

"I'm sorry," Solo apologised. "I didn't see you there."

"No, you never do; now stop it before you knock us both off!" Storm demanded. She had little sympathy for her blind mother. *What good is a blind cat?* she often asked herself. Sadly, Solo knew her daughter didn't have much love for her, but she never blamed her for it. She had been far too young when she gave birth to both Storm and her larger twin brother, Casper. Although, Solo had tried her very best, her young age and sudden blindness had made it difficult for her to care for them as much as she would have liked. It had taken years for Solo to learn how to cope with and adapt to the loss of her sight. So, at a very early age, both Casper and Storm had needed to largely fend for themselves. Solo knew that no one could love Storm as much as she did and hoped that one day her daughter would forgive her for what happened to her brother.

"Sorry, nearly found it," Solo responded.

"Found what, exactly?" Storm enquired, as she grew increasingly impatient with her mother's fidgeting.

"The perfect spot. Ah, there it is," Solo explained, and then she settled down for a well-earned snooze. Solo hated being blind, but she was a lot stronger constitutionally than she looked. She had to be, otherwise she would never have made it to her ripe old age. However, that didn't mean things couldn't hurt her; thinking about Casper again, hit her hard. She could never forgive herself for not being able to see the white van speed towards Casper that fateful morning all those years ago. Her torment from Storm being so angry at her had made Solo even more resolute to cope with her visual impairment and dedicate her whole life to being there for Storm. If only her daughter would realise that, then perhaps she would be able to forgive Solo.

It took little time for both of them to fall soundly asleep, even though they were lying too close to one another for Storm's liking, and Solo was so upset at how much she missed Casper. Instead, Solo reminded herself of how Bracken had become her adopted son. Sure, it wasn't ideal having a smelly dog that was far too big and clumsy to be a mother to, but she knew Bracken loved her, and she loved him. Even though he never remembered that she was blind and often bounded into her, scaring her half to death. Tonight, she would get to sleep, consoling herself that at least Bracken loved and respected her, even if her daughter didn't.

The wind was getting stronger, causing the cat flap in the back door of the house to constantly bang open and shut. Grant never forgot about the broken catch on the cat flap; he said he just kept forgetting to put it on his daily 'to-do' list. Whilst Solo and Storm were used to it banging when it was windy, tonight it was swinging harder than it had ever done. Eventually, the noise was loud enough to stir Storm from her slumber. Drearily, she climbed off the cushion and went to investigate. As she made her way to the back door, she took a sip of water from the dish Grant had topped up when he was making his and Alison's bedtime drinks that evening. Storm was grateful that whilst there were a few things Grant forgot to do because they weren't on his 'to-do' list, making sure there was always enough water for her and Solo wasn't one of them. Grant never forgot their water.

As Storm sat and stared at the swinging cat flap, she wondered if this was the worst weather she had ever seen. She recalled it had been particularly bad last year but neither her nor Solo had been around to see it. Grant had insisted they both went to stay with the children; who were, of course, all grown up now and living in other villages. Grant had said cats shouldn't be near a river when it's raining very hard. Although, Storm had hated leaving her home, she hated water even more and since the house was eventually flooded, she was grateful Grant had sent them away.

Despite the noise of the swinging cat flap, Storm was suddenly distracted by the sound of her mother bumping into a chair leg. "Oops, sorry," Solo apologised to the chair, as she tentatively fumbled her way past it. Normally, Solo was very good at navigating her way around the house by remembering reference points throughout each room. Occasionally though, furniture had been moved, which usually caught her out. Storm often wondered how many more times her mother would bang her head before she got some sense.

Storm instinctively said, 'Tsk, tsk!' and rolled her eyes at her mother's clumsiness.

"What are you doing, Storm?" Solo asked when she heard her daughter.

Storm didn't answer her mother, instead she turned back to staring at the swinging cat flap. Unperturbed by her daughter's hostility, Solo slowly made her way towards where the 'Tsk, Tsk,' had come from. As she reached Storm, she sat beside her and stared in the general direction of the banging cat flap. "It sounds bad," Solo said, trying as ever, to break the silence that often fell between her and Storm. "I don't remember the weather ever sounding as bad as this," she continued. Storm remained silent; growing increasingly worried

about the weather. "Should we wake Grant up?" Solo asked.

"No, let them all sleep," Storm replied. "He'll only worry if you wake him." Solo smiled; it was nice to get a response from Storm, even if she didn't agree with it. At least she'd broken the awkward silence between them. They continued to sit in silence, but it wasn't an awkward one; there just didn't seem anything appropriate to say that didn't include how bad the weather was getting.

Suddenly, there was a rumbling sound from beneath them.

"What was that?" Solo asked.

"I'm not sure," replied Storm. Just then a loud hissing sound started coming through the floor and began to surround them.

"It sounds like something is leaking," Solo proclaimed. Then, without warning, the floor below them seemed to move. "We're moving!" Solo shrieked as the whole house began to rise upwards!

If there is one thing cats hate more than water, it's when the floor beneath them begins to move. Storm reacted, leaping towards the back door and pushing open the cat flap to make her escape. She stopped suddenly when in front of her she saw a huge brightly-coloured wall that rose up from what appeared to be a red cushion underneath the house. "What is it?" Solo asked when she noticed Storm wasn't exiting through the cat flap.

"I'm not sure," Storm answered. Whilst she never usually paid any attention to Grant's engineering antics,

Storm had to admit it looked remarkably like what she'd seen rolled up on the cellar floor, when she'd recently snuck down there to investigate the 'secret' project Grant and Bracken had been so busy working on. Bewildered by the array of bright colours which now surrounded her, slowly, she climbed through the cat flap. Storm couldn't stop herself; instinctively she knew she had to find a secure place that wasn't moving in order to assess their situation further.

Once outside, Storm's back arched, and her ears tucked into her head when she came into contact with the heavy rain that was falling. Then, her tail retreated between her legs as she felt the wobbly floor beneath her. She didn't like walking on it one bit; she had to find a way to more solid ground. Slowly, she walked around the side of the house.

"Storm?" Solo cried. There was no reply from Storm. Solo knew she had to follow her; there was no way she was going to let her daughter wander off on her own with the weather as it was.

Carefully, Solo followed Storm, clambering through the cat flap. She had no idea where she was once she'd got beyond the back door, as she didn't recognise the feel of the wobbly ground beneath her. For no other reason than to seek shelter, she chose to turn left, away from the driving rain coming from the west. Keeping as close as she could to the side of the house, she felt her way round to where she recalled the side passage was. Cautiously, she crept towards what she assumed was the front of the house, but everything seemed very different to how she remembered it.

The rain was hammering down hard, and the wind was howling as it squeezed itself through every nook and cranny down the side of the house. Solo kept close to the building as she tried desperately to gain what protection she could from the elements. As she emerged around what she thought was the front of the house, the wind and rain hit her hard. She could hardly hear Storm shouting,

"Over here!" her daughter called out from somewhere in front of her and to her right. Slowly, Solo made her way towards where Storm's cry had come from. She struggled to keep upright as the rain soaked the slippery surface beneath her, which was now moving about even more vigorously. Solo soon became disorientated and cursed her blindness as she realised she had no idea where she was.

"Call again!" she cried out to Storm.

"Over here!" Storm called back to her. "I'm over here," she shouted again and then again. Storm kept shouting, as she watched her mother changing direction and begin heading towards her. "Stop!" Storm suddenly shrieked, as Solo reached the edge of the slippery red floor beneath her. "I'm sat on the garden wall at the front of the house," Storm told her mother. Solo knew the place well, she often liked to sleep on it during the summer. It wasn't a high wall but high enough to keep Solo safe from Bracken's enthusiastic tail-wagging.

But now, the wall seemed to be in a very different place to how she remembered it. Solo recalled that if Storm was actually on the wall then she should be directly in front of her and not off to the side. "Over here!" Storm cried out again when she saw her mother struggling to orientate herself.

"You've moved again," Solo called back. "Stay still, so I can focus on where your voice is coming from," she instructed her daughter.

"I'm not moving!" Storm called back, "It's you who's moving, or rather the house is," she informed her mother.

She's moved again, Solo thought to herself.

"You should go back inside the house; it's too dangerous," Storm suggested.

"Why is the house moving?" Solo shouted back.

"Because it's floating... on the water," Storm informed her. It was a long enough reply to allow Solo to home in on Storm's position, and so, Solo immediately threw herself off the house and sprang as hard as she could in the direction of her daughter's voice.

"Nooooo!" Storm screamed, but it was too late. Just as Solo sprang into action, the house spun around as it floated on the turbulent waters of the River Thames that now surrounded them. Solo desperately hoped that her enhanced senses as a result of her blindness, would serve her well and take her in the right direction.

Her senses were indeed finely honed and had served her well over the years, but even they were fallible under such extreme circumstances. Had the house not turned at that last second, she would have made it, but instead, sadly, 'SPLAT!' She collided into the side of the wall and fell head first into the freezing, turbulent currents below. "Muuummm!" Storm screamed as she saw her mother disappear below the water.

Storm was furious that her mother had ignored her advice, as she sat on top of the wall with her arms folded in the habitual pose that she always adopted in order to express her disgust at her mother's disregard for safety. Then, as quickly as it had all happened, her frustration soon gave way to a feeling of utter desperation when she realised the seriousness of what had happened to her mother. Storm had never felt as helpless as she did at that moment. She had never imagined feeling like she did, unable to bear the thought of losing her mother. Yes, she wondered what was the purpose of a cat that couldn't even see a chair leg until it hit her. And of course, she blamed her mother for what happened to Casper. But she loved her mother, and a life without her would be even more terrifying than water.

Chapter 2
Moving Home!

As Storm sat grieving her loss, the raging currents grew in strength and pushed the water higher up the wall towards her. She feared that soon she would have to find another safe place, but the prospect of moving further from her home filled her with fear. Just then, she noticed the house was already further away from her than it had been; her home was drifting away. *What on earth?* she asked herself. *Where's the house going? What has Grant done now?* In a matter of minutes, Storm was losing everything; losing your mother is bad enough but having your home leave you as well is ridiculous. She had no choice; as much as she hated water, she needed to be in her home, now more than ever before.

Without hesitation, Storm decided she would leap off the wall onto the log which was floating towards her in the wake of her moving home. As she crouched wiggling her bottom in preparation of jumping, she couldn't help but recall the fateful jump her mother had made only minutes earlier. She would have only one chance to catch the log and there was no room for error. *Not yet, not yet... Now!* she told herself as she jumped as recklessly as Solo had done, out over the raging water below her.

Thankfully, despite not having thought out her plan as thoroughly as she would have liked, Storm's feline instincts and nine lives had been enough to ensure she made it onto the log as it floated past. Although, no cat likes to admit they may have used up one of their nine lives, even Storm had to agree it was a miracle she hadn't ended up in the freezing cold water like her poor mother.

Storm had no idea where she was heading, as the log she clung to kept changing direction and speed in the raging current, colliding with one obstacle after another as it went. Holding on for her life, Storm became overwhelmed with everything that had just happened, as she thought about her mother and watched her home disappearing into the distance. It was all too much for anyone to bear, even someone as seemingly cold-hearted as Storm. She began to cry, something she hadn't done for a long time, not since Casper had his accident. Louder and louder she cried, like she'd never sobbed before, as the log carried her in pursuit of her home.

"Storm! Is that you I can hear?" a weak voice cried out from the darkness ahead of Storm. She stopped crying, wondering if she was imagining things. "Storm?" the weak voice called out again, closer this time but sounding weaker.

"Mum?" Storm called back, "is that you, Mum?"

"Over here!" Solo beckoned, so quietly that Storm could barely hear her. A few metres away in the darkness, she could see a drowned rat-like form, clinging desperately to a fallen tree. Quickly, Storm laid on her stomach and dangled all four of her paws into the freezing cold river either side of the log. She had

never experienced a sensation as unpleasant before, but without hesitation, she started paddling the log towards the fallen tree and her mother.

"I'm coming!" Storm cried, as she struggled to hold back her tears of joy at discovering that her mother was still alive. Sadly though, the warm emotion from knowing Solo was safe lasted only as long as it took Storm to manoeuvre the log and her now tired and sickeningly-wet body to where her mother clung to the tree, where most of Solo's body was submerged below the icy cold waters. "I told you not to jump!" Storm rather coldly chastised when she reached her stranded mother. "Why didn't you stay with the house?" Storm asked.

"Sorry," Solo replied, "Jumping seemed a good idea at the time, when the house was moving." Instead of being relieved that her mother still had her sense of humour, Solo's calmness only served to drive out the last trace of compassion her mother's near-death experience had stirred in Storm.

"Well, don't think that you're my responsibility," Storm coldly informed her mother, with even less sympathy than she might show a stranger begging on the street, which is very little.

"Can you reach this log?" Storm asked. Tentatively, Solo released one of her paws, which had dug its claws deep into the trunk of the fallen tree she clung to and reached out in the general direction of Storm's voice. Desperately, she waved her paw around hoping it would connect with the log. At least twice she became fully submerged in the rapidly flowing icy waters before she finally made contact.

"Well done!" She heard her daughter call out. "Can you bring your other leg across?" Storm asked. After brief consideration as to whether or not she had any of her nine lives remaining, Solo let go of the tree and prayed she could make it to the log.

"Yes!" Solo screamed as she felt her claws dig firmly into the side of the log.

"Aaaargh!" shrieked Storm when the pain registered in her brain as Solo's claws embedded in her leg.

"Sorry!" Solo apologised.

Once her mother had wearily pulled herself onto the log, a familiar silence soon descended upon them. Storm returned to her paddling position on the log and began steering them both towards drier land above the water. Storm cursed under her breath at her wet and now painful leg as she paddled. Solo hoped her daughter wasn't looking at her, as she tried desperately to stifle a smile; she hadn't meant to hurt Storm, but you had to admit it was quite funny. Solo's urge to smile soon wore off as the bitter cold began to numb her soaking wet body.

Fuelled with anger at her pain and intolerance of her mother's incompetence, it didn't take Storm long to paddle their floating log to a nearby wall and forget that she had nearly lost her mother. "We should get off here," she suggested as she manoeuvred the log to allow Solo to pull herself on to the wall. Once her mother was safely off the log, Storm joined her. Tired from the freezing cold and their near-death experiences, they both gingerly made their way along the top of the wall towards higher ground. Eventually, they stopped on top of a neighbouring garage roof and sat a moment in familiar silence until Solo spoke. "Can we go home now?" she asked.

As often happened when Solo asked a question, Storm didn't answer her mother. Instead they continued to sit in silence. Finally, Storm replied, "Well, you'll need to go and find it before you do," she said.

"Find what?" Solo asked.

"Our home… It's gone! You'll need to go and catch up with it if you want to go home," Storm clarified, as she cursed that only her mother could have missed something as crucial as their home drifting off in the flood.

This time Solo didn't respond; she didn't know what to say. Instead, Solo did what she usually did to cope with the adversities of life she frequently had to face, she settled herself down as cats often do. Not lying but not sitting either, her front paws were tucked in under her chest and her rear legs were bent so she was ready to spring into action at a moment's notice if required. Solo began to purr.

"What on earth have you got to purr about?" Storm challenged her.

"Nothing! Sorry," Solo quickly replied, startled at Storm's tone of voice. Needless to say, silence once again descended upon them, both too cold and exhausted from their recent ordeals to have any suggestions as to what they should do next. Instead, they held their respective positions far enough apart for Storm's liking but close enough to know what each other was doing.

As the rain continued to fall and the wind picked up speed, Solo silently edged closer to her daughter in search of any additional warmth she could get. It was freezing cold even for Storm who, being larger than her mother, had a somewhat thicker layer of insulation. Eventually, Solo had got a little too close for Storm's comfort, "Okay, I am going to look for our house," Storm suddenly announced. "You should stay here," she told her mother.

"I'll freeze if I stay here all alone," Solo replied.

"Well, you should have thought about that before you ignored my advice and jumped off the house. At least you would have been dry and warm if you had stayed there," Storm informed her.

"I could help you look for it," Solo offered.

"What, you?" Storm asked, rather bemused at the idea her mother could find anything, even a floating house!

"Well, I'm not staying here on my own," Solo insisted. She regretted not having stood up to her daughter more during their lives together and was determined to do that from now on.

Surprised by her mother's insistence Storm said, "Okay, but don't expect me to take care of you."

Solo's heart broke at her daughter's words. It had been broken many times in her life, as she was frequently reminded that she'd not only lost Casper that fateful day, she had lost both her children. Solo dearly wished her daughter could see past her tainted opinion of her mother and realise just how much she was loved. With so much water around and the cold weather, Solo knew her visual impairment was likely to be an even greater burden than usual, but she was determined to help her daughter find their home. Of course, it would be difficult, especially when Storm didn't even want her there, but then life had always been difficult for Solo.

Storm lead the way, and Solo followed as closely as she dared without annoying her daughter. She remained just close enough to be able to accurately follow Storm's footsteps. Relying on her finely tuned senses of hearing and smell, Solo also had her unwavering trust and belief in her daughter's ability to find their home.

Gradually, they climbed higher above the water, which continued to rise, forced by the relentless flooding of the river ahead of them. Carefully, Storm walked a course along the rooftops of the adjacent houses that lined the road where their house used to be. Taking advantage of their elevated position, Storm surveyed their intended course in the direction their home had drifted. She was fully aware they were much higher up than she would ever choose to be. *But in reality*, she told herself, *I'm only a metre higher than the water level, so it's not that high up at all*, she reassuringly concluded.

Not forgetting who was hot on her heels and unperturbed by the raging currents of the flooded river ahead, Storm plotted her rooftop route, taking care to avoid any large gaps between adjacent houses. For once, their luck seemed to be holding as they kept crossing from one rooftop to the next all the way down to the riverside. Storm unexpectedly stopped dead in her tracks; sadly, their luck had run out. The larger, more expensive houses lining the River Thames had the benefit of more spacious gardens and meant it was too far for Storm to jump from one rooftop to the next, let alone her mother.

"Oops, sorry!" Solo apologised, as she stumbled into her now stationary daughter in front of her. Storm said nothing; she just stared ahead trying to think of what to do next. "Why have we stopped?" Solo eventually asked.

"We've run out of roofs," Storm informed her. "Our home floated into the river and down that way," she said, pointing in the direction the river was flowing. Then, realising her mother couldn't see where she was pointing, she added, "We need to follow the flow of the river."

"Like in a boat?" Solo asked.

"Yes, a boat would be good. I don't suppose you've seen one, have you?" her daughter enquired sarcastically, confident she already knew the answer.

"Sort of," Solo unexpectedly replied, "if you could guide us back to the house two doors down from where our house used to be, I think they have one on their garage roof," her mother said. "I sometimes shelter under it if I'm locked out, and it's raining."

"You mean when it's raining like tonight?" Storm asked, "How long did we sit on that garage roof getting soaking wet, and you never mentioned this?"

"You never asked me. Besides, I thought with all this water around, it would probably have floated off somewhere, like our house did," Solo pointed out. Storm just stared at her mother, incredulous that she hadn't thought to mention the shelter earlier.

"Perhaps it did float off, but it's worth checking anyway," Storm decided, as she turned and retraced their tracks back towards the house two doors down from where theirs used to be. On reaching what Storm calculated must have been the house Solo had described, she announced, "We're in luck, the boat's still there," resisting the urge to shoot off ahead to investigate further, remembering that she still had her mother-in-tow.

As luck would have it, the upturned kayak was still where Solo had said it had been, and more importantly, it was still intact, complete with paddles. Thankfully, luck was back on their side. Storm instructed Solo, "Stand here and when I say push, lean as hard as you can against this end of the kayak, and I'll push the other end."

Gradually, they edged the heavy kayak over the sloping garage roof into the water only a metre below them. As Storm held tight to the kayak's rope, she instructed her mother, "I'll hold onto the rope, so it doesn't float off, whilst you jump in."

"Where am I jumping into?" her mother asked. "Wouldn't it be better if you jumped in first? That way, you can call out to me, so I know where to aim for?" Solo, suggested.

"Like last time, you mean?" Storm asked. "Because that didn't go very well, did it?"

"But I'm not having to contend with a moving house this time, am I?" Solo pointed out.

For the first time in her life, and just for a minute, Storm was immensely proud of her mother's uniqueness. Despite her earlier failed attempt to complete a jump, here she was determined that this time would be different. Solo's apparent disregard for her disability and eternal determination convinced Storm this wasn't an argument she should try and win. Instead, for the first time Solo could remember, her daughter agreed with her suggestion and handed her the rope.

"Please hold tight to the rope!" Storm told her mother.

After some hesitation, despite being no more than a metre below her, Storm leapt off the garage and straight into the front cockpit of the two-seater kayak. Storm knew her mother was considerably thinner than her but that aside, she also knew that such a feat was extremely difficult even for a cat that could see, never mind a blind one, even if she was smaller. "Are you sure about this?" she shouted to her mother as she manoeuvred the kayak closer to the garage wall. "Only, I am sat in the front cockpit, and you now need to aim for the rear cockpit, do you think you can do tha—?"

Before Storm had even finished her sentence, Solo had already launched herself fearlessly off the garage roof towards where her finely tuned senses told her to aim... taking into account water movement and the dimensions of your average two-seater kayak... not! "Aaaargh!!!" Storm screeched when her mother's claws instinctively in defence mode, struck her on her head and back as Solo landed in exactly the same place where Storm was sitting.

"Sorry!" Solo apologised.

"Get off me!" Storm demanded, as she pushed her mother towards the rear cockpit of the kayak and began nursing her wounds. Keeping her back to Storm so her daughter wouldn't see her smiling, Solo positioned herself in the rear cockpit.

"You're facing the wrong way," Storm informed her mother as she turned to lick her head and back wounds. "I think under the circumstances, I should be the one at the front, don't you?" Storm asked. Solo's shoulders started to shake as her smile had now developed into an unbearable desire to laugh. Solo couldn't speak; she just remained facing the wrong way, her shoulders shaking being the only sign of emotion. Storm wondered if her mother was perhaps crying, as she should be for what she did. So, Storm dropped the conversation and returned to facing the front, leaving her mother to reflect on her irresponsible actions.

Again, the familiar silence descended on our intrepid duo, as Storm came to terms with her latest set of wounds and muttered under her breath something about being cursed by a useless mother. Or at least that's all Solo could make out from her mumblings. Solo hadn't meant to land on her daughter like that. *It's not easy being visually impaired,* she reminded herself. *I did my best, and at least I made it this time without almost drowning again*, she reassured herself. She didn't like that she'd hurt Storm again, but she had to admit, it was quite funny. She wished one day her daughter would stop taking life so seriously. After all her mother didn't, and what could be more serious than being a blind cat!

Solo curled up the best she could in the wet cockpit of their boat and began her usual purring.

"Must you?" Storm asked her mother.

"Must I what?" Solo enquired, unaware she was doing anything wrong.

"Purr like that; it's annoying, and it's keeping me awake," Storm informed her.

"Sorry," Solo apologised, accepting that perhaps it wasn't necessary for her to purr, considering the current circumstances.

As they both crouched in silence, sheltering from the elements in their respective cockpits. They soon succumbed to the day's challenges, as tiredness took over them, and they fell soundly asleep.

Chapter 3
Go with the Flow!

Solo and Storm both knew they would soon have to wake up to face a new day and with it, face their on-going challenge of finding their missing home. But neither of them expected the time to pass so quickly. Solo was the first to stir from her deep slumber; she stretched her legs and opened her eyes wide as her highly tuned senses of hearing, touch and smell began to stir. Although the darkness that had accompanied her whilst she slept still remained as it always did, Solo began to interpret her surroundings. The rain had stopped and the ever-so-slight warmth she sensed suggested that it was a clear day with the sun shining as best it could in the middle of winter, struggling to barely rise above the horizon.

Solo sensed they were moving, but she had no idea where they were. However, she could allow herself some solace in the knowledge that they were still afloat at least. "We're moving!" she called out to Storm, who began to stir in her cockpit at the front of their boat. It didn't take Storm long to be fully awake. As usual, she didn't answer her mother, instead she froze, spellbound by their unfamiliar surroundings.

"Where are we?" her mother enquired, hoping that her daughter wasn't still mad at her about the 'jumping in the kayak' incident the night before.

"I don't know…" Storm replied. "But we're definitely moving…" Suddenly without warning, the front of the kayak was grabbed by a raging current ahead of them, which spun them around and around, faster and faster.

"I don't like this!" Solo screamed as she instinctively tried to dig her claws into the hard-plastic body of the kayak to prevent herself from being thrown out.

"Hold tight!" Storm screamed as the front of the kayak was pulled down into the turbulent water which engulfed them. Solo's senses were already in overdrive, as she tried to assimilate what information she could in a desperate attempt to orientate herself to what was happening. A challenge for anyone, visually impaired or not, given the circumstances. It was made even harder by the fact that Solo was still facing the wrong way in the kayak, and therefore, now travelling backwards, at great speed. Again and again, Solo was lifted up into the air with the rear end of the kayak each time the front dived below the water, as they were tossed by one cross-current after another.

"I feel sick!" Solo cried, as if there was even the slightest chance that anyone could do anything about that. Quickly, they gathered speed as the cross-currents turned the kayak and carried it eastwards in its escape towards the open sea, somewhere far in the distance.

Not surprisingly, neither Storm nor her mother had any idea where they were heading. They both clung on for their lives, desperately hoping their journey would end soon. For fifteen kilometres, they clung on, waiting for the forces that were hurling them down river to subside. But the force was relentless; the waters that Storm had assumed were the river at the end of their road bore no resemblance to any river Storm had seen before. Instead, their surroundings resembled something more akin to the wild, open sea. The river had long since breached its banks, spilling its contents out into the surrounding terrain, submerging the whole area in water.

Buildings either side of the river were flooded, fields were nowhere to be seen, and even the bridge which spanned the river ahead of them was only a few centimetres above the surface of the turbulent water.

That's what we should do! Storm suddenly thought. *We'll grab onto the bridge when we reach it,* she assured herself. Then, as often happened, she reminded herself that her mother would have no chance. Instinctively, she turned her head to look at Solo who was still facing the wrong way in the kayak. For a brief but real moment, Storm cursed the burden her mother's blindness placed on them both. They would have to think of another way to stop their transit downstream, which was taking them further away from where their home used to be.

Suddenly, for no obvious reason, they began to change direction as the kayak started to turn left towards where the riverbank used to be. Storm noticed the flooded buildings were rising higher out of the water than they had been. Either the water was getting shallower or the buildings were getting taller, she surmised. *There must be a way to stop the kayak,* she repeated to herself over and over, hoping to come up with a solution. Gradually, their craft steered against the currents towards the taller buildings. *How can that be?* Storm asked herself. *What is changing our direction and pushing us away from the stronger currents?* she wondered.

"Where are we going now?" Storm barely heard her mother ask from the rear of the kayak. Solo was leaning out of the cockpit over the rear of their kayak and was talking to the river!

"Who are you talking to?" Storm enquired, assuming that her mother had finally lost it. She'd always suspected blindness wasn't Solo's only affliction. For years, she was convinced her mother had dementia or 'catzheimers', which Storm often insensitively referred to it as. Talking to herself was just one of the many tell-tale signs of old age her mother displayed, as well as purring at the most inappropriate times and walking into chairs.

"Thank you," she heard her mother call as she sat back into her cockpit. "We're going to be fine," her mother shouted, in the general direction of Storm.

Storm considered politely ignoring her mother's gibberish but couldn't stop herself from toying with her, as she asked, "Why are we going to be fine?" in a sarcastic manner.

"Our friends are helping us," her mother replied, bemused by her daughter's inability to see what was happening. Even a blind cat could see they had clearly slowed down and were turning away from the stronger currents.

"What friends?" Storm probed, unable to resist an opportunity to make her mother look even more stupid than she already did, still sat facing the wrong way in the kayak.

"I'm not sure, I forgot to ask them," Solo confessed.

This'll be good, Storm thought to herself. If their situation hadn't been as grave as it was, she might even have broken into a smile at the prospect of teasing her vulnerable mother again.

"They clearly like water, and they smell an awful lot like fish, but they feel furry," Solo offered, hoping that might be enough for her daughter to know what they were. "Oh, and they make a low purring sound, like me!" she added proudly.

"Unless it was a washed-up, hopeless cat like you, that sounds a lot like a river otter," Storm informed Solo, somewhat relieved that perhaps her mother hadn't totally lost it… just yet! "You know, you really need to ask what someone is when you're talking to them, and you're blind!" Storm scolded her mother.

"I remember Bracken telling me about otters in the river once," Solo recalled, not meaning to say it out loud.

They were both so engrossed in trying to figure out who was helping them that they hadn't been paying attention to where they were heading. Slowly, the kayak wove its way between the tall buildings that rose out of the flood water and high into the clear, blue sky above them. "Where did our home go?" Solo asked, suddenly changing the topic of their conversation, as she often did.

"What?" Storm asked, incredulous that anyone, even her mother, could relate a question like that to what they had just been discussing. *From otters to missing homes? Only my mother's catzheimers brain could work that way,* she said to herself.

"Where did our home go?" her mother asked again, when Storm didn't answer.

"I don't know," Storm told her. "It just drifted off."

"How?" her mother asked.

"It was surrounded by a bouncy castle, you know, like the one our next-door neighbour's daughter and her friends bounced on all of last summer," Storm reminded her.

"What colour is it?" her mother asked as if it were an obvious question.

"What has that got to do with anything?" Storm enquired.

"In case we have to ask someone if they have seen it. We need to be able to describe what it looks like," Solo pointed out.

Only her mother could think there might be more than one house drifting around… wherever they were!

"Where are we?" Storm asked, when she suddenly realised they hadn't been paying attention to where they were going. They were stationary in a wide stretch of water between two very large buildings. The building on their right had clocks on it near the top, and the one to their left looked a lot like the church in their village, only bigger, much bigger. Storm had no idea what the huge church was, but she did recognise the clocks on the tower.

"I think we're in London," she said bemused.

"What? London, as in London?" her mother asked, not quite sure what she meant by that, but it didn't matter, Storm was ignoring her anyway. Solo decided not to correct the question she had just asked. Instead she kept quiet and allowed her daughter time to survey their surroundings in the hope that she would come up with a plan as to what they should do next.

It's at times like these that I hate being blind, Solo conceded to herself. Her highly tuned senses were now overwhelmed with all the new smells and unfamiliar sounds they had encountered recently, and all the twirling around in the kayak had left her totally disorientated. She had no choice but to admit that Storm would have to be the one to work out where they were. *But together, we will figure out a way to get back home*, she promised herself.

Their silence didn't last long. "We didn't say goodbye!" Solo couldn't help blurting out.

"What?" Storm snapped, having been distracted from her efforts to determine their whereabouts and likely route home.

"To the otters?" Solo reminded her rather sheepishly, as she realised she had just interrupted her daughter's train of thought. Storm just shook her head and returned to surveying their surroundings.

"We should have at least said thank you," Solo muttered to herself as she huddled in the rear cockpit of the kayak, trying the best she could to shelter from the icy cold air that surrounded them. What little sunshine the winter allowed during that clear day was well out of sight behind the big buildings that surrounded them. Solo's senses informed her that darkness would soon be descending. She wasn't sure she would last another night in the cold, damp kayak.

"We need to find somewhere to shelter," Storm eventually announced, much to Solo's relief.

"Do you know where we are?" she asked Storm.

"Not exactly but I think that might be Big Ben," Storm explained, instinctively pointing towards the clocks on the building beside them before realising that pointing was no use to her mother. "I think that is Big Ben standing tall on our right," she informed her mother.

Now Solo was worried; not only were they lost but, *Now, my daughter has got catzheimers*, she thought to herself. *Either that, or there are some incredibly tall people living in London.* Solo remembered talking to someone once, who had been to London, but she didn't know what they were because she had to confess, she'd forgotten to ask. She promised to herself that in future, she would not forget to ask what someone was and consoled herself in the knowledge that whoever they were, at least she knew it hadn't been an otter; she could never forget the fishy smell of an otter. Anyway, whatever it was, they had never mentioned anything to Solo about incredibly tall people living in London. Some undesirable people maybe but not particularly tall ones.

"You'll need to face the other way now!" Storm instructed her mother. "We need to paddle ourselves further into the city and find some drier land," she said, as she positioned herself in the front cockpit. It was a stretch, but Solo turned herself round and leaned far enough over to her right, so that her paw reached the water. "Uuurgh!" she said, when her paw made contact with the icy cold water.

"You paddle on that side when I tell you," Storm directed her before leaning as far as she could herself, over to the left. Storm resisted the urge to repeat her mother's reaction when her paw also connected with the freezing cold water. "Now paddle!" she ordered her mother.

Slowly, they meandered down narrow streets as Storm alternated between sides of the kayak in order to steer their course. Gradually, they paddled their way, unbeknown to them across Parliament Square Garden and turned left into where Birdcage Walk would normally have been. Then they turned right, across a large, boating lake that used to be St James' Park. They continued past the Imperial War Museum to the right, over The Mall and then across Pall Mall, passing Trafalgar Square on their right. Storm had no idea where they were going, she just hoped she might see something that she recognised; after all, they were in one of the most visited cities in the world. It was just a pity neither she nor her mother had been one of its many visitors before it flooded.

"Are we there yet?" Solo cried out as her tired arms were no longer able to move; numbed by the icy, cold waters and stiffened with excessive use. *No cat is designed to paddle for this long*, she argued to herself. *Come to think of it, cats aren't designed to paddle at all!* "Can we stop now?" she pleaded with Storm.

"I don't recognise anything," Storm confessed, "I hoped if we paddled long enough, I would see something familiar, but everything looks so different to the images of London I've seen on the television."

Suddenly, right on cue, her despair was lifted as the sky in front of them lit up with the unmistakable haze emanating from the bright lights of the infamous advertisement screens in Piccadilly Circus. "Just up here!" she encouraged her mother, "Come on, paddle!" she cried, as their extreme introduction to kayaking also took its toll on her. Painfully, Storm turned their kayak left up lower Regent Street towards the somewhat familiar and strangely warm feeling, Piccadilly Circus.

It was the most surreal experience as the two cats emerged into the eerie silence of the normally bustling hub that is Piccadilly Circus. There was no one home, yet all the lights were on, which strangely made Storm think of her mother. As they stopped paddling, absorbed by their spookily quiet surroundings, they were both suddenly brought back to reality when their kayak abruptly ground to a halt outside what Storm recognised as the famous, Lillywhites sports emporium. Not that either of them was in any mood for cricket, or any other sports for that matter, but at least it was a familiar place, and it looked dry. Well, most of it at least!

"We should stay where we are for the night," Storm suggested, as she eyed the six-storey building which towered above them.

"What, you mean we should sleep in the kayak again?" her mother asked, "It's freezing and cramped in here," she pointed out in case her thick-skinned daughter hadn't noticed.

"Well, we could try and get inside that huge building," Storm said. "But it doesn't exactly look as if the place is open for business," she pointed out to her mother.

"There's always a way into a building, and the bigger the building, the more ways there are to get in," Solo argued. "Your Uncle Horace always said so."

"And who exactly is Uncle Horace?" Storm asked, not really sure if she even wanted to know the answer.

"You know Uncle Horace, he was my brother's friend," Solo reminded her.

"Your brother's friend! I never even knew who my father was, how on earth would I know who Uncle Horace is?" Storm snapped back. Solo fell silent, not really knowing what to say to that. Storm had made a good point, and she knew she talked too much at times.

"Go on then, I give up. Who exactly is Uncle Horace?" Storm asked, no longer able to tolerate her mother's silence for a change.

"He was a cat-burglar, the best in the business, apparently," Solo informed Storm, "There wasn't a building built that your Uncle Horace couldn't get into if he wanted to. He used to say that for every entrance in, there were at least two exits out, you just had to find them," Solo told Storm.

"Genius!" Storm exclaimed. "So, we either contend with a sooty chimney, or we fight our way through an air-conditioning duct, is that it?" she asked patronisingly.

"No, we look for opportunities," Solo calmly explained.

"You, look? Fat chance you'll see anything!" Storm cruelly reminded her mother. *She did have another good point,* Solo conceded, *but I'm not about to give up without even attempting to find somewhere warmer than the kayak to spend the night.*

Slowly, Solo prised herself out of her cockpit. "Where are you going?" Storm asked. Her mother, uncharacteristically, didn't reply. Carefully, Solo lowered her back legs over the side of the kayak. The water was freezing cold and dangling her paws in it was the last thing Solo wanted to do right then, but she was glad she had.

The water was no more than six centimetres deep. She almost smiled when she realised.

"It's not deep at all!" she spoke out.

"What?" Storm asked.

"The water, it's not deep at all, look!" her mother replied. Only the shallow keel of a kayak could have allowed the two of them to have travelled in such shallow water before running aground.

Typical, Storm thought. *Goodness knows how long we've endured our extreme introduction to paddling a kayak, when we could have been wading through the water instead.* But never mind. *At least now,* she consoled herself, *we don't need to spend another night in the kayak.*

Storm didn't take much convincing before she followed her mother out of the kayak and led the way, wading towards the Lillywhites sports emporium. If Uncle Horace was correct then, with any luck, she might just get a dry night's sleep, and who knows, she

might even pick up a new Tottenham Hotspur football shirt at the same time!

Chapter 4
London's Underground!

"This way," Storm called to Solo. "We should go around the back and check out the entrance for deliveries," she suggested. Unfortunately, the delivery door was well and truly locked, but as luck would have it, every window that could be opened had been left open as wide as it could possibly go. "Wow, take your pick," Storm said as Solo joined her at the rear of the premises. "They must have left all the windows open to help dry out the flooded ground floor. Which one should we go through?" she asked.

"I guess we should choose whichever window is closest to the ground," her mother replied, as she stood shivering, up to her knees in the freezing cold water.

"Yes, of course," Storm acknowledged, admitting to herself that she'd momentarily forgotten about her older, fragile, thinner-skinned and, of course, blind mother.

"You don't like heights, remember?" Solo reminded her.

"Quite," Storm replied after a little hesitation, unsure if she should be offended or not by her mother's remark.

"Follow me!"

It took Solo some time to pluck up the courage and strength to leap up onto the lowest windowsill, where her daughter patiently sat, repeatedly saying, "I'm just here." Over and over again she called, so that Solo's disorientated senses could home in on the direction she needed to jump. But finally, she made it and, much to Storm's relief, there were no wounds inflicted this time.

Both Storm and Solo were too tired to explore their new surroundings; instead, they quickly took up comfortable positions on two piles of sports clothing which were next to each other. The air around them was damp and cold but at least they were sheltered from the biting wind that was blowing outside. Solo didn't even carry out her 'getting comfortable' routine, as she quickly curled up in a ball, burying her cold nose under her paws.

Storm decided to adopt the 'ready for action' position as she lay with her back legs bent and front paws tucked under her chest, just in case. Within seconds of them both settling down, Solo began her habitual purring. *Here we go,* Storm sighed to herself.

"Why was it there?" Solo suddenly asked.

Oh, even better, another random conversation! Storm said to herself. "Why was WHAT there?" she asked her mother, desperately wanting to be left in peace so she could get some sleep.

"The bouncy castle, under our home," Solo replied, as though it was obvious what she meant.

"I don't know, maybe Grant put it there to prevent the house flooding. Don't forget, he used to be an engineer. Now can we please get some sleep?" Storm pleaded, too exhausted to argue with her mother.

"Oh yeah…" Solo said. "But why?" she pressed.

Storm decided it would require less effort to ignore her mother rather than try and explain one of Grant's many, random engineering projects, so she adopted her usual silent treatment approach to Solo and said nothing.

"Well, if Grant put the bouncy castle there, surely he would have fitted something to our home so that it didn't just drift off like that," Solo pointed out.

"Maybe 'fitting a retaining device' was a job like 'fixing the broken cat flap' and wasn't on Grant's 'to-do list.' NOW CAN YOU PLEASE STOP TALKING SO I CAN GET SOME SLEEP?" Storm yelled at her mother.

"Sorry," Solo apologised, as she closed her eyes and began to purr again.

It was strange, but for the first time she could remember, Storm actually enjoyed hearing her mother purr next to her. She found it warmly reassuring, as she quickly drifted into a deep sleep, blissfully unaware she was laying on a pile of Arsenal F.C. football shirts.

It had been an uneventful night when Storm eventually stirred the following morning. In fact, Storm couldn't remember having ever slept as soundly as she had that night. It was just beginning to come light by the time she finished licking herself clean and rubbing the sleep from her tired eyes. *Boy, I'm hungry,* she thought to herself, suddenly realising that neither of them had eaten for at least two days. Storm needed to find something to eat, but she didn't fancy anything a sports shop might have to offer.

Storm decided to leave Solo sound asleep; she could scour their adjacent surroundings for food quicker without her mother to slow her down. With any luck, she would be back before Solo woke up and she could bring some food for her. Storm slipped quietly out of the open window they had come through the evening before.

"She's gone!" the ring-leader rat whispered from where he lurked in a corner of the shop floor. He and his two fellow rogues had been patiently waiting in the shadows for their opportunity.

"Are you sure?" the thin rat asked. "Only, I didn't like the look of the younger one; she looked temperamental to me."

"So, how should we do this?" the big-boned rat asked the ring-leader. "Shall we knock her out, or should we suffocate her, with one of those football shirts she's lying on?" he asked.

"We don't want to damage her," the ring-leader rat pointed out. "We need her alive, let me think a minute."

"Well hurry up, I think she's waking up... Look!" the big-boned rat noticed.

"Storm?" Solo asked as she stretched her legs and shrugged off her drowsiness. "Storm?" she asked again when her daughter didn't answer. She wondered if perhaps she'd talked too much the night before and that, as usual, Storm was giving her the silent treatment. There was still no reply, Solo tentatively felt over the edge of the pile of Chelsea shirts she was sitting on, unable to remember how far off the floor she was.

"What's she doing?" the thin rat asked. "Why doesn't she just jump off, isn't that what cats do...? And she's sitting on a pile of Chelsea shirts, how disgusting is that?"

"Shhh!" the ring-leader cautioned, "I think she might be blind."

"BLIND!? Who ever heard of a blind cat?" The big-boned rat asked in disbelief.

"Who's there?" Solo asked, alerted by her highly sensitised hearing which had picked up the rodent's comment.

"Shhh, she can't see us, but she sure can hear us," the ring-leader rat pointed out.

"We're friends!" the ring-leader called back to Solo from the shadows.

"Oh, that's a relief," Solo replied, "I was worried there for a minute."

"Blind and stupid, by the looks of it," the big-boned rat said under his breath.

"Shhh... We're here to help you," the ring-leader rat said as he stepped out of the shadows and walked towards Solo.

"I don't know where my daughter has gone," Solo told him.

"That's why we're here," the ring-leader rat said to her. "We're friends of your daughter and she asked us to make sure we took you to her; she's gone to find some food for you," he explained.

"Oh, okay, is it far?" Solo asked.

"Not that far, follow us," the ring-leader instructed her as he headed towards the open window.

"Where are you?" Solo asked.

"Crikey, she's seriously visually impaired!" the thin (and somewhat politically correct) rat pointed out.

"Keep quiet! And just whistle so she will know where we are," the ring-leader rat ordered his two rodent colleagues.

"Whistle what?" the thin rat asked.

"What about 'Three Blind Mice'?" the big-boned rat suggested.

"Oh, I know that tune," Solo said.

"She is seriously impaired..." the big-boned rat whispered to the thin rat, "in more ways than one."

Happily whistling 'Three Blind Mice,' the big-boned rat led the unlikely quartet as they made their way out of Lillywhites and into the urban wilderness of the deserted streets of Piccadilly Circus. Solo was blissfully trustful of her new 'friends,' who she innocently believed were taking her to have breakfast with her daughter. "This is going even better than I hoped," the ring-leader rat whispered to his thin rat colleague as the four of them marched through the deserted streets, looking as though they were carrying out a bizarre re-enactment of the Pied Piper of Hamelin.

It didn't take them very long to reach dry land and the temporary headquarters of Greedy Fat Cat who was the evil boss of the underground crime world in London. Normally, you might expect to find a crooked greedy fat cat, in the Docklands; but because of the floods, he had been forced to move his underground money-making operations to drier ground in Soho. "Look what we've brought you, Boss," the big-boned rat couldn't resist shouting out, once Solo had passed the threshold to their temporary HQ, and the door had been slammed shut behind her.

"Ah, boys! What have we got here?" Greedy Fat Cat asked.

"She's bli—" the big-boned cat started to explain, before the ring-leader rat elbowed him in the stomach and cut him off.

"Let me handle this!" he butted in. "I think she could make you lots of money, Boss," the ring-leader rat began to explain, "I reckon we could put her to good use, begging on the streets of London."

"Begging? A cat? Who has ever heard of a cat begging?" Greedy Fat Cat asked. "Cats never beg!" he said firmly. "This cat's different; she's old, fragile, lost… and she's also blind!" the ring-leader rat informed his boss. "And I think she might have catzheimers!"

"Blind…? She is indeed a different type of cat," Greedy Fat Cat agreed. "Is she expensive to keep?" he asked.

"I doubt it, Boss, judging by how skinny she is," big-boned rat chimed in.

"Excellent, we have to keep in mind my profit margins, you know." The evil boss of the city's underground crime world reminded them all.

"I don't beg!" Solo, corrected the ring-leader rat.

"Is that right?" Greedy Fat Cat asked, as he walked round Solo, eyeing up his latest ill-gotten gains. "You will be begging, when I've finished with you... FOR YOUR LIFE!" Greedy Fat Cat enlightened her.

"Put her in the guest room," he instructed his loyal devotee rats. "You've done well, boys, we'll put her to work in Mayfair after breakfast. The streets will be drier up there, and we all know how much money people in Mayfair have, don't we, boys?" he told his loyal followers; as usual, putting food before everything else!

As Solo sat down in the dark and smelly prison cell which Greedy Fat Cat referred to as the 'guest room', she faced the wall. No longer able to orientate herself to the unfamiliar surroundings, she began to purr as Solo always did whenever she wasn't talking.

"Is she purring?" the thin rat asked the big-boned rat as they listened outside the door.

"Yeah, I think she is... Wow, that is one seriously crazy cat!" the big-boned rat replied, as the two of them laughed and headed off to re-join their evil comrades.

"What's for breakfast?" the big-boned rat asked. "Nothing, Felix isn't here yet," the ring-leader rat informed him.

"Ah Felix, there you are! About time; you're late!" Greedy Fat Cat said to the young fox who had just arrived. "What have you brought us to eat?" the big-boned rat asked.

"Not much," Felix said, once he dropped the part eaten, extra-large 40-centimetre, deep-pan, stuffed crust, pepperoni passion pizza, with pineapple, which he had been carrying in his mouth.

"Uuurgh, pineapple!" the big-boned rat exclaimed, "Who puts pineapple on a pizza? Humans are so disgusting."

"You're going to have to do better than this, Felix, if you want me to keep up my end of our agreement," Greedy Fat Cat warned the young fox.

"It's been difficult to find food recently because of the flooding; half my territory is still under water and there are fewer people around to provide their discarded, uneaten food," Felix informed him.

"You'll lose more than half of your territory, Felix, if you leave me no choice but to flood it with thousands of rats from my underground, crime operations," Greedy Fat Cat threatened Felix. "You know what will happen when your pathetic territory becomes overrun with thieving rats; they'll bring in The Exterminators... and we all know how much they hate foxes, don't we?"

"Yeah, even more than they hate rats," the thin rat agreed, proudly.

"The Exterminators will just chase off my rats, but they will kill you, Felix," Greedy Fat Cat reminded the young fox. "Now, you'd better start looking further afield for food Felix; we'll be starving by dinner time

with these paltry offerings you've brought us for breakfast."

"Is there no limit to your greed?" Felix asked the Greedy Fat Cat.

"No, why, should there be?" Greedy Fat Cat replied, much to the amusement of the rat trio.

Sadly, Felix had to concede that even a wily young fox couldn't educate the blind ignorance of the Greedy Fat Cat from Docklands, who was the mastermind behind London's corrupt underground crime world.

"And no pineapple, next time!" the big-boned rat shouted when Felix turned to leave them. Felix hated being at the mercy of Greedy Fat Cat and his rodent disciples, but he had no choice. Greedy Fat Cat was right; if the pest control people were to come, it would be the end for Felix. He had no choice but to fulfil his blackmailer's demands. As he went outside, Felix desperately hoped that if there was any justice in the world, with any luck they'd all choke to death, greedily guzzling down their food.

Felix sat high on a nearby wall looking at his half-flooded territory and resigned himself to having to search for food beyond his territory, if he was going to satisfy the fat cat's greed. But that would mean invading another fox's territory, and Felix didn't like that. Fighting to defend his own territory was one thing, but picking fights to steal another fox's food would mean he was no better than the villains he despised so much.

'Talking of whom...' Felix said to himself, as he noticed the three rats accompanied by their boss, dragging a poor cat on a lead through the street below.

What are those despicable crooked rodents up to now? he wondered to himself, as he stood up and began to follow them across the rooftops. He was certain they would be up to no good, whatever they were doing, and Felix didn't like that, especially on his territory!

Chapter 5
Beggar's Belief!

Storm had spent longer than she had intended, looking for food for herself and her mother. There had been a couple of discarded, half-eaten kebabs lying around, but she was a domesticated cat, and domesticated cats have standards. She was missing her home now more than ever. But her patience had paid off handsomely, and she had found a discarded pile of recently-expired, pre-packed sandwiches behind one of the shops. She'd selected two; one with tuna and sweetcorn for herself and another with ham and cheese, for Solo.

As Storm climbed in through the open ground floor window of her temporary new home, a sense of overwhelming loss suddenly engulfed her as the absence of Solo's purring instantly struck her. "Mum?" she asked having dropped both the sandwiches she was carrying in her mouth. "Mum?" she called again, louder this time. There was no reply. *Where could she have gone?* Storm quizzed herself, "Surely, she didn't go looking for me, did she?" she said out loud. *How could my mother have found her way out?* she wondered. Frantically, Storm scoured the ground floor of the department store, which was no mean feat when you consider the size of it. She was convinced her blind mother could not have made it out of the building unaided and, so, must be somewhere inside. Quickly, she ran up the first flight of stairs and searched the first floor, then the second floor, third floor and fourth floor, but still nothing. Solo was nowhere to be seen. Storm was desperate. Whilst she had believed her mother could not have made it outside unaided, her common sense was telling her Solo definitely wouldn't have made it up so many floors. Storm's imagination began to run wild, as she suddenly considered, *What if someone had come to the department store to check on it, such as a security guard, and had found her mother asleep and taken her somewhere?* Storm pledged to herself that she had to find Solo.

Storm was grateful that running down the four flights of stairs was far easier than it had been climbing up them. But her legs were weakening. Going up the stairs, Storm had been fuelled by the adrenaline caused by the worry for Solo. Having not eaten in two days, what little energy she had was deserting her, now that the adrenaline had run out. She panicked as the reality of having mislaid her blind mother began to set in. With greater effort than she would have liked, Storm climbed out through the open ground floor window to continue her search outside. She had no idea where to look for Solo, but she had to start somewhere.

***

"This looks like a good spot, boss," the big-boned rat said once they had reached Grosvenor Square, close to the Millennium Hotel in Mayfair. "There's loads of money around here."

"Good idea. Tie our beggar to those railings," Greedy Fat Cat instructed his wicked accomplices.

"I told you before, I am not a beggar!" Solo tried to correct him.

"You are today, my dear," the ring-leader rat informed her. "Here, put these sunglasses on and shut up."

"Don't expect me to do anything for you lot," Solo spat out in defiance.

"That's the beauty of being a beggar... you don't have to do anything; just stay here and do nothing, other than be yourself. I'm even beginning to feel sorry for you... not!" Greedy Fat Cat told her. His rodent followers found this very amusing.

"Here, hang this cardboard notice round her neck, and give me that white stick you stole off that old woman the other day," ring-leader rat instructed the big-boned rat.

"There, that looks perfect!" the thin rat said, putting the sunglasses on Solo as the final touch.

"Now, you stay right here; we'll be watching your every move." Greedy Fat Cat warned Solo.

"But my daughter will be worried about me," Solo pleaded, as she changed tactics, hoping to appeal to any grain of compassion her evil captors might have.

"Daughter?" Greedy Fat Cat asked, as he looked at his villainous crew and wondered why none of them had

mentioned this important point to him before. When none of the rats were forthcoming with an explanation, Greedy Fat Cat seized the opportunity to exert even more pressure on Solo to ensure she conformed with their unscrupulous demands. "Don't you worry about her; as long as you keep up your end of the deal, your daughter will be safe…" he threatened Solo, "but if you don't, who knows what might happen."

"What do you mean?" she asked.

"We have her securely locked up, and if you don't do as you are told, you'll never see her again. Not that you can see her that well anyway, ha, ha." Greedy Fat Cat insensitively mocked poor Solo, much to the delight of his rotten gang of rodents.

"Now, come on boys, let's leave her to make us some money. And remember, my dear, we'll be just across the street, watching your every move, so get begging!" Greedy Fat Cat warned, as the four of them skulked off, leaving Solo feeling hungry and desperately alone.

"Unbelievable!" Felix muttered quietly to himself from his vantage point on the other side of Grosvenor Square, where he sat watching the events unfold. "It beggars belief that even a soulless, wicked scoundrel like Greedy Fat Cat could stoop so low as to carry out this latest act of evilness," Felix said in total disbelief. Seeing the poor, helpless cat looking so vulnerable at the mercy of the gangsters was more than Felix could bear. But unfortunately, he had his own problems to deal with, and eventually Greedy Fat Cat and his gang would be expecting to be fed again.

When Felix could no longer watch Solo, he reluctantly conceded he had no choice but to stay out of this and resume his efforts to deliver on his own grossly unfair burden imposed on him by the unscrupulous and downright evil Greedy Fat Cat and his underground crime ring. He headed off towards the fox territory adjacent to his. Perhaps, there he would find enough food to satisfy his blackmailer's greed, for another day at least.

"Do we really have to stay here and watch her?" the big-boned rat asked his boss.

"Of course not, you boys can go and do what it is you do to make me more money, and I will go and, erm… do what I do to make me more money," Greedy Fat Cat said, fully intending just to go back home and sleep off his breakfast. "We'll come back and get her later and see how much money she's managed to make for us."

***

Storm had no idea where she was; she had changed direction time and time again, frantically searching one winding street after another. The fading, winter daylight and surrounding tall buildings had restricted her ability to keep track of her bearings. She had no choice but to admit she'd lost her mother, and now she was also hopelessly lost, in a city she neither liked nor wanted to be in.

Eventually, her tired legs refused to move anymore; the cold and damp proving too much for them. Storm hated the dark, and nightfall was looming close; she was lost and all alone, which was more than her normally strong constitution could handle. As she sat staring into the metropolitan wilderness, she began to cry. If only she wasn't scared of heights, like any normal cat, she would be able to travel quicker between the sprawling buildings. If only she wasn't afraid of the dark, she could keep looking for her mother, like any normal cat. And if only her mother was a normal cat, she wouldn't be in this desperate situation in the first place.

Why did mum leave the department store? Why didn't she just wait for me to return? Why did mum not stay on the bouncy castle like I told her to? were just some of the questions racing through Storm's mind as she burst into tears and cried inconsolably.

I wonder what's wrong with her? Felix asked himself when he spotted the crying cat from the rooftop he was sitting on. "It's none of your business, Felix," the young fox told himself out loud. But it was his business; she was on his territory, or rather, she was a convenient excuse for Felix to put off the inevitable fight he would have to endure if he carried out his intention to trespass on his neighbour's territory.

"Are you okay?" Felix asked, once he had made his way down from the rooftop to where Storm was sitting.

Sniff, sniff! "Sorry?" Storm asked, as she stopped her sobbing and wiped away the tears with her paw.

"Are you okay?" Felix repeated.

"I don't think that's any of your - *sniff* - business - *sniff* - do you?" Storm replied defiantly.

"Probably not," Felix muttered to himself, as he turned to retreat, sensing he wasn't welcome.

"Please don't go!" sniffled Storm. "I'm sorry, that was rude of me. I can't – *sniff* - help myself sometimes," Storm explained.

Felix sat down at a safe distance, waiting for further encouragement that the stranger wanted him to speak. She didn't want him to speak; just his presence was all that Storm needed. She hated being alone in a strange city. Even a smelly fox was company in such a lonely place. Felix could do silent; he often sat for hours alone in his favourite vantage point, not speaking to anyone, just surveying the city skyline. He could stay quiet no problem if it would help the sad stranger. He felt sorry he hadn't done more to help the other poor cat earlier; perhaps, he could make amends by at least being there for this one. Besides, staying where he was had to be better than getting into a fight with his neighbour.

"My name is Storm; do you live here?" Storm eventually asked, turning around to look at her visitor.

"I'm Felix, and yes, I do live here; this is my territory," the fox replied.

"Territory... What do you mean?" Storm asked.

"I'm a fox, in case you've never seen one before, and we all live in territories," Felix explained.

"Of course, I've seen a fox before. I just didn't know you all had territories," Storm responded.

"Sorry," Felix said, "I didn't mean to sound patronising. You look as if you've got enough problems without worrying about my fox wit."

"No, it's fine. I'm sorry I'm so defensive, I'm just… lost!" Storm confided, realising that the young fox probably assumed cats were never lost, normal cats that is.

"That's okay," Felix reassured her. "I get lost all the time!" he said, hoping it might make her feel better.

"I don't believe that for a minute," Storm replied.

"Ha ha, well, maybe I don't," Felix conceded, "at least not on my own territory. So, tell me, how have you come to be lost?" Felix asked, moving closer to Storm so he could see her face.

"It's a long story," Storm told him.

"Try me! I've nothing better to do tonight," Felix said.

"Well, my home drifted off on a bouncy castle!" Storm said. "How's that for starters?" she asked him, testing the water to see whether or not the young fox could handle the truth as to why she had come to be lost. "Do you know what one of those is?" Storm asked, when Felix didn't react.

"Of course, I know what a home is!" Felix replied, which made Storm laugh. "And I know what a bouncy castle is." Felix quickly added, before joining in on Storm's laughter.

"I take it the recent floods had something to do with your home drifting off, but you'll have to help me understand the bouncy castle part," Felix said, when they'd both stopped laughing.

"Yes, the floods did cause that, but only because of the bouncy castle. I'm not certain, but I think Grant, he's one of my owners by the way..." Storm clarified.

Owners? Felix wondered. *Is her home, a zoo?* Felix considered, perplexed by the idea of being owned by someone!

"Do go on," Felix encouraged Storm.

"I think Grant, he used to be an engineer you see, adapted the bouncy castle and fitted it under our home to ensure it wouldn't flood again, like it did last year," Storm surmised.

"Surely, if Grant used to be an engineer, he would have fitted something to prevent your house from drifting off like that... would he not?" Felix asked.

"Well, you'd think so, wouldn't you? But there you have it; that's why I'm here, lost and all alone in London," Storm concluded, unsure she wanted to tell the stranger much more about her personal circumstances. Besides, he probably didn't believe what she'd told him anyway, she wouldn't have, had she not seen for herself their home drifting off like that.

"Wow," Felix said, "That's a cool story. Tell me, does the bouncy castle have red, green and yellow horizontal stripes and four purple vertical towers, complete with blue turrets on top?" he asked.

"Yes!" Storm answered, "Have you seen it?"

"No, it must have been a lucky guess...! Of course, I've seen it," Felix joked. "How else could I have described it so accurately. I saw it when the flood was at its worst here... drifting up the River Thames and

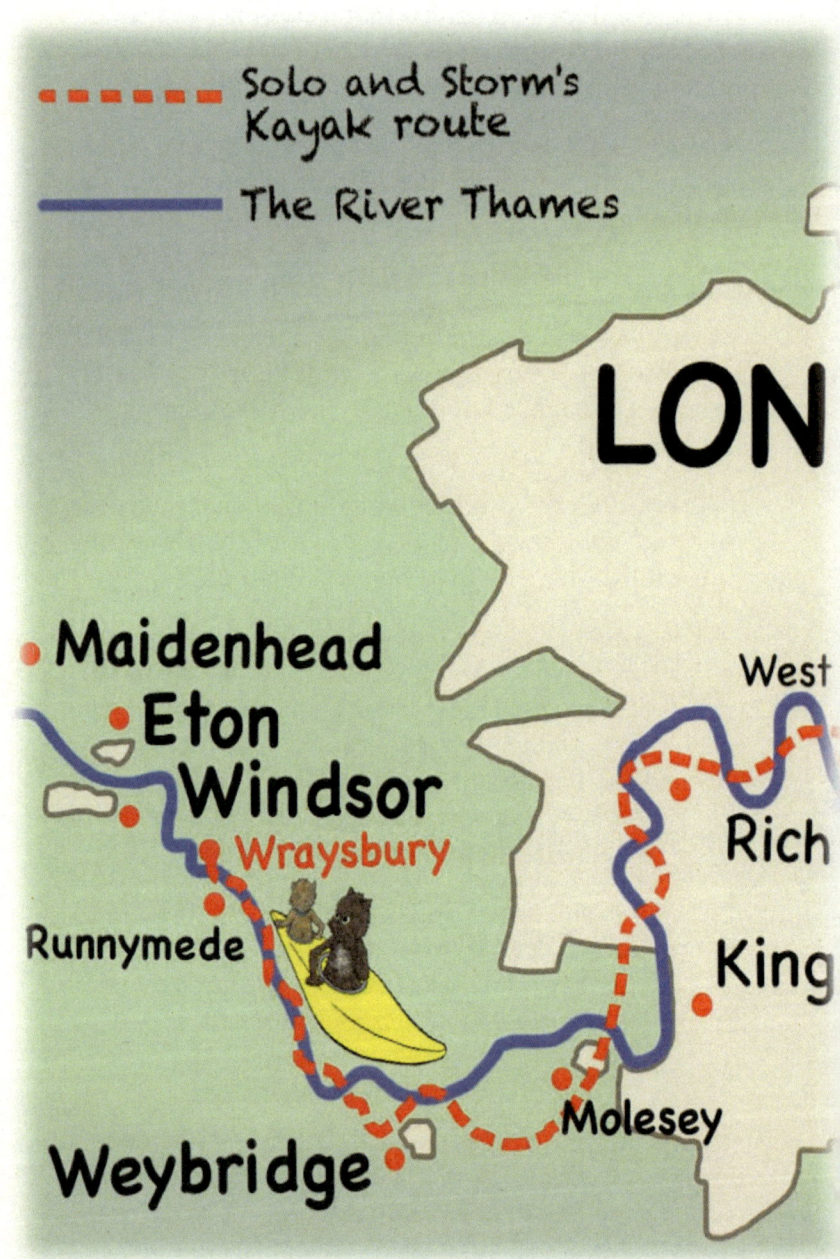

heading west. Were you on the bouncy castle?" Felix asked.

"No, not then, that's another long story...for another day. But that's good news that you saw it; they must have been heading back home... if you know what I mean," Storm surmised.

"Back to your territory you mean?" Felix asked.

"Yes, I suppose so," Storm agreed.

Felix nodded, that was indeed good news. No one should leave their territory vacant for long, or someone might steal it, like he was shamefully being forced to do.

After they both sat there for a while, trying to make sense of everything that had happened and what was still happening, Storm announced, "I need to find my mother."

"Your mother?" Felix asked. "Don't tell me, she's lost too? Sorry, I couldn't resist that. What does she look like, maybe I've seen her?" he asked. "I consider it my responsibility to know when anyone is on my territory," Felix explained.

Felix's heart sank, as Storm described her fragile, old and blind mother who also suffered from catzheimers.

"I know where she is," Felix told her.

"You do? That's great!" Storm responded. "Let's go and get her," she suggested, rising to her feet.

"It's not that simple," Felix said. "We'll need a cunning plan if we're going to successfully rescue your mother," the young fox told her.

"Rescue her?" Storm asked. "Is she in danger?"

"No, not now that we know where she is. I have a plan," Felix reassured her. "Have you eaten today?" he then asked Storm.

"No, I haven't eaten for a few days now. But I know where there are some sandwiches if you could guide me back to Piccadilly Circus," she said.

"Follow me," Felix responded, as he led the way. He needed time to fine tune his cunning plan to rescue Storm's mother from the clutches of Greedy Fat Cat. If Storm had indeed found some food, he could fulfil his daily commitment to the villains and delay a visit from The Exterminator, for one more night at least, and buy himself some time. *That should be long enough for a wily young fox like me to come up with a perfect rescue* plan. Felix reassured himself.

It didn't take Felix long to lead Storm back to Piccadilly Circus, since it was familiar territory, one he'd spent all his life getting to know, and he knew every shortcut there was. Ordinarily, he wouldn't have believed Storm could have discovered some food on his territory that he wasn't aware of. But he had to admit he had been neglecting Lower Regent Street, to the south of Piccadilly Circus because of the flooding. But now, the amount of water was much less, so perhaps Storm had found some food.

Storm took over the lead, once she recognised her surroundings and led them straight to the sandwich stash she had discovered.

"Well done," Felix congratulated Storm. "Wait here for me but go ahead and eat without me. I have an errand to run," he told her before selecting as many pre-packed sandwiches as he could carry in his mouth. *Six should do, even for those gluttonous villains*, he convinced himself, as he reluctantly headed off to feed their insatiable appetites.

Chapter 6
Rich Pickings!

Storm didn't have to wait long before Felix returned. Having to interact with Greedy Fat Cat twice in one day was more than Felix could tolerate for long. He despised the evil antics of the gangster cat and his motley rodent crew. Delivering their sandwiches gave him the opportunity to make certain Storm's mother was indeed being held captive in their temporary headquarters. He was adamant that he would devise a cunning plan to free their vulnerable prisoner and spare Storm's mother the further torment of the rogues' appalling hospitality. Greedy Fat Cat was obviously pleased with his day's ill-gotten gains and would no doubt be inflicting further torture and humiliation on Storm's mother by forcing her to go begging again tomorrow.

"Is everything okay, Felix?" Storm asked, sensing the young fox was distracted.

"Er, yes, no problem," he replied. "Have you eaten?" he asked Storm.

"No, not yet!" she replied, having politely waited for her new friend to return. Felix encouraged Storm to pick whichever sandwiches she would prefer, saying he wasn't fussy and could eat anything.

As they each consumed their respective sandwiches, Storm couldn't help but notice the feline characteristics the young fox displayed as he delicately bit off small chunks of his roast chicken and stuffing feast sandwich. Like many of us, she had always assumed foxes were more canine than feline, but close-up, that wasn't the case.

"Have you lived here long, Felix?" Storm asked when she'd swallowed what was in her mouth.

"It's the only place I've ever lived," Felix said.

"Wow, you must like it here," Storm suggested.

"It's home," Felix said. "Sorry, I shouldn't have said that when you've just lost your home," he added, when he noticed Storm's head drop and her polite smile disappear.

"It's okay, I know you didn't mean anything by that," Storm reassured him. "Don't be offended, but I can't say I like what I've seen of this city so far," Storm confided. "I prefer the countryside, which is not surprising I guess, considering it's the only place I've ever lived too. It's all I've ever known," she confessed.

"Have you had enough to eat?" Felix asked.

"Yes, I think so," Storm replied.

"Come on then, I want to show you something," Felix said, as he stood up and waited for Storm to follow him.

"Where are we going?" Storm asked, hesitant at being led away from the only part of London she recognised.

"It's not that far, follow me," the young fox said.

Once again, Felix led the way as Storm followed him down a series of narrow streets until they reached a tall building with an old wrought iron staircase at one end. *Please tell me he's not going to climb up that,* Storm pleaded to herself. She was frozen to the spot when Felix began to climb the stairs.

"Are you okay?" he asked.

"No, not really. I hate heights!" Storm confessed, "You must think I'm crazy."

"No, I don't think you're crazy," Felix told her. "A fear of heights is one of the most common fears there is."

"But I'm a cat. Have you ever heard of a cat being afraid of heights?" she asked.

"No, I haven't," Felix confessed. "Do you know for sure that it's the height you're frightened of, or are you frightened of falling?" he asked.

"What do you mean; aren't they the same thing?" Storm probed.

"Well, if it's the height you're frightened of, I have to admit it's quite high up there, and I wouldn't expect you to follow me. But if you're frightened of falling, I can promise you I won't let that happen."

Storm had never thought of her dislike of heights like that before. "I'm not sure which I'm frightened of," she had to admit.

"Good," Felix said, "then we must find out, so we can try and help you conquer your fear. Come on." He encouraged her. "You can lead the way, and I'll follow you. Trust me, it'll be worth it."

Storm liked Felix and appreciated that he wanted to help find her mother, so she didn't want to disappoint him. She cursed her phobia of heights and surprised herself by leading the way.

"That's it," Felix encouraged Storm as she tentatively began to climb the stairs. "I always come up here when I need to devise a cunning plan; I find it helps me think," Felix continued, as they ascended. "You asked me if I liked living here, so I thought I could do two jobs at the same time; come up with a cunning plan so we can rescue your mother, and also show you something that I hope you will agree is well-worth seeing," he continued, stopping for a second to catch his breath. He never usually talked very much and especially not when he was climbing seven flights of stairs. "What's your mother's name?" he asked, "No, don't tell me, let me guess; Sheba?"

"No," Storm replied.

"What about Tiger?" Felix pushed.

"Ha ha, of course not," Storm laughed.

"Kitty then…? No wait, I know, Jemima," Felix tried again.

"No," Storm laughed, "You'll not guess it."

"Wait a minute, I know, I bet her name is Princess," he tried again.

"Princess? Who on earth would call their cat Princess? That's old school! Come on, you're not even close," Storm teased him.

"Well, it must be Snuggles then." Obviously, Felix was getting desperate.

Just as Storm was about to correct Felix again, he announced, "Look, you've made it!" Storm suddenly realised she had reached the top of the staircase. In front of her was a large flat roof with a small ledge all the way around it. Instinctively, she grabbed hold of the handrail of the staircase.

"You won't fall off," Felix assured her as he passed her and went out onto the rooftop. His most recent cunning plan had worked brilliantly; he had distracted Storm so much with all his incessant babbling and name guessing that she didn't even notice how high they were climbing. "Come and look at this," Felix beckoned her.

She felt unusually calm considering she was so far from the ground below. As she made her way towards where Felix sat, she gazed out over the magnificent London night skyline that stretched out before them.

"This is where I live, Storm," Felix pointed out once she'd sat down beside him. Storm looked awestruck by the stunning view. "I'm afraid you can't see much countryside, but I can think of far worse places to live," he said. "I often come up here just to remind myself that there's more to this city than meets the eye at street level."

"Thank you," Storm said.

"Thank you for what?" Felix asked.

"For helping me up the stairs, so I could see this," she said.

They sat in silence for half an hour taking in the view. Both of them lost in their own thoughts about how Storm could be reunited with her mother.

"We will get your mother back," Felix eventually announced reassuringly.

"Her name is Solo," Storm informed him, realising Felix never intended being able to guess her name. He was just distracting Storm whilst she climbed up the stairs.

"Good plan," Storm said.

"You don't know what my plan is; I might not have come up with one yet," Felix replied.

"No, not your plan to rescue my mother, the one you used to get me up those stairs," Storm explained. "Very cunning."

"You're welcome," Felix replied proudly.

"Tell me, what would you have done if I'd panicked and freaked out?" she asked.

"Oh, I had another cunning plan if that had happened," Felix assured her.

Storm just looked at him, expecting Felix to enlighten her.

"I could tell you what that plan was, but then I'd have to kill you," Felix said, as he smiled and winked at Storm.

"Do you have parents?" Storm asked Felix.

"I did, but my father was knocked down by an Uber taxi when I was very young, and he died. My mother struggled to bring me and my two sisters up on her own. Then she left home, taking my sisters with her when I was seven months old," Felix told her.

"I'm so sorry, Felix," Storm said sympathetically.

"It's okay, at least she waited until I was old enough to take care of myself. She said they were leaving so that I could have our territory to start my own family in. My mother always said the city was no place for single vixen foxes to live, so the females all left. I think secretly she wanted to go back to the countryside where she was born. So, that's why I am still here, trying to hold on to the territory my mother so generously gave me. But it's not easy, what with the flooding and all the greedy crooks around here. Which brings me to your mother," he said, as he turned to face Storm.

"Do you have a cunning plan yet?" Storm asked.

"I'd thought of one before I forced you up here," Felix said. "That's why I needed to help you to overcome your fear of heights."

"Oh really, just what do you have in mind?" Storm asked, growing increasingly anxious about what her role might be in his cunning plan. Felix wanted to spare Storm the gruesome details about the suffering and humiliation her mother was enduring at the hands of Greedy Fat Cat and his evil rodent trio. He knew, though, that she needed to appreciate the seriousness of Solo's predicament in order to secure her full commitment to carrying out her crucial part in his cunning plan.

"Unfortunately, your mother is being held captive by a ruthless, gangster cat and his underground crime gang," he told her. "She's okay at the moment, but I am worried what might happen if she becomes no longer of financial benefit to them," he warned.

"Financial benefit?" Storm asked. "I don't think she's earned any money in her life." ...*Like me,* she admitted to herself.

Felix didn't wish to tell Storm they were abusing her mother by forcing her to beg for them in the more affluent tourist destinations of the city. Instead, he told her, "I'll spare you the details. Suffice to say I would prefer to prevent them from doing the same to her tomorrow as they did today. To do that we need to act very early tomorrow morning."

"Go on," Storm urged Felix, still anxious to hear her part in all of this.

"We will need something irresistible to lure the crooks away from their headquarters, rich pickings so valuable they will be unable to resist pursuing them. I will need you to use those rich pickings to lure them away so I can rescue Solo. As long as you evade capture by the villains, we will meet up again at a rendezvous point outside Paddington Station, where your mother and I will be waiting for you. Then you will be free to resume the search for your home and hopefully the crooks will have no idea that I helped you," Felix concluded.

"That sounds like a good plan to me Felix," Storm said relieved that her part in it sounded like it just entailed her running away a lot.

"I'm afraid it's not without risk, Storm," Felix said solemnly. "These are evil creatures who you must make absolutely sure never catch you. Running to Paddington will require you to memorise a route that I have marked out for you, and it will mean you dealing with your fear of heights, as you'll need to successfully negotiate a number of rooftops. Do you think you're up to that?" he asked.

"She's my mother, Felix. What happened to you has reminded me I should treasure having my mother in my life. You can count on me to do my very best," she assured him. "Thank you, Felix. I think it is indeed a brilliant and cunning plan, worthy of any wily fox."

Felix smiled and returned to enjoying the view. They sat silently staring into the night sky, each of them absorbed by their crucial roles the next day.

"What makes you think the villains will find me so valuable that they are willing to risk their lives chasing me across rooftops?" Storm eventually asked.

"No offence, but it won't just be you they will be after. It will also be what you're wearing," Felix said. "I will take care of providing the necessary bait. Trust me," he reassured her. "Tell me about your family Storm," Felix asked.

"Well, you know my mother, and I'm afraid I never knew my father; neither did my mum, apparently. So, there's not much to tell," she replied, sadly remembering how dysfunctional her family had been.

"You had no brothers or sisters?" Felix probed.

"I had a twin brother, but he died when we were both still very young," Storm confided.

"Do you remember anything about him?" Felix asked. "What was his name?"

"I do remember him, every day. I think of him at least once; his name was Casper," Storm said, as she smiled and turned to face Felix.

"You know, you remind me of him in some ways," she told him.

"I'm assuming he couldn't possibly have been a fox, so do tell me more," Felix enquired.

"Well, he was bigger and much cleverer than me; he was always working on a plan. However, on the other hand, he was nothing like you. He was totally white, and one of his eyes was blue, and the other was orange," she recalled.

"Wow, he was a special cat then, like your mother?" Felix asked.

"Ha ha, yes he was. He also used to drink water out of a dripping tap in the bathroom, by jumping into the sink," she smiled, as she recollected the many crazy things her twin brother used to do, before his untimely death.

"I'm so sorry you didn't have more time together," Felix said softly. "You must miss Casper a lot."

"I do," Storm agreed, suddenly realising that she had just talked to someone about her brother for the first time, and even more remarkably, she hadn't blamed her mother for what had happened to him.

After sitting for a little while longer, enjoying the view, Felix suggested that they needed to go. "We have an early start in the morning," he said. "You should get some rest."

Storm could only agree; conquering her fear of heights had been tiring work. Carefully, Felix led the way back down the stairs as Storm tentatively followed behind, concentrating on making sure she didn't put a paw wrong.

"Well, that was a lot easier than when we went up, well done!" Felix said, as Storm stepped onto the street. "Come on, I'll take you back to Piccadilly Circus," he said before leading the way.

"This is my place," Storm announced, when they reached the Lillywhites sports emporium.

"Nice place you have!" Felix said, as he eyed up the impressive six-storey building.

"Please wait here; there's something I need to give you," Felix said as he sped off down the street. He returned quickly, carrying a roll of paper in his mouth which he dropped at Storm's feet. "Here, take this," he said, pawing the rolled-up street map towards Storm. "I've marked two escape routes on this map which will take you to Paddington Station; one via the streets, the other over rooftops. Solo and I will be waiting for you at the station. Memorise whichever route you would prefer to take, it will make it easier for you tomorrow" he advised her. "I will meet you back here first thing tomorrow morning, before daybreak."

"Thank you, Felix," Storm said, picking up the map in her mouth and retreating back to her home for the night.

Chapter 7
Mind the Gap!

Solo had hardly slept at all, despite being exhausted by her introduction to begging the day before. Perhaps she may have slept if she hadn't been so hungry; Solo reckoned it must have been at least four days since she last ate, but she couldn't be certain. Her first night in the villains' guest room had been just as disorientating as her first night in the city. It was near impossible for her to keep track of time. The cold and damp of her prison cell meant the hours she was held captive there passed very slowly, and the hours she was forced to beg seemed even longer. She wondered if Storm was okay and whether she would be searching for her mother. As her lack of sleep and food played havoc with her imagination, she even wondered if Storm had abandoned her in the sports shop, knowing that she would have a better chance on her own of finding their home, without her mother's blindness and frailty to slow her down.

Still Solo purred, despite her fears, the sound echoing back at her as it bounced off the cold stone walls that surrounded her. She tried desperately to make sense of all the thoughts racing through her mind but to no avail. *What if Storm is injured somewhere? Or what if she's also been kidnapped by the evil gangsters? Or maybe, just maybe… she found our home and is safely curled up on Grant's lap, in front of a warm fire.* Solo chose to hold on to the latter possibility. Undoubtedly her ability to think like that contributed to her amazing capacity to cope with the many challenging ordeals that life had unfairly thrown at her.

***

It was still dark when Storm heard Felix calling through the open window at the back of Lillywhites. She hadn't slept much at all; she was too worried about what the day had in store for them. She was grateful Felix had given her two route options; she wasn't sure her nerve would hold that long to escape via the rooftops.

"How are you this morning?" Felix asked, as Storm climbed through the open window to join him outside. Storm never liked early starts on cold winter mornings, and that morning was particularly cold. It was pretty much still night in Storm's opinion.

"Nervous," she informed Felix.

"Good, that'll keep your wits sharp," he said, as he smiled reassuringly. "I'm sure you will be fine."

"I don't want to let you or my mother down," Storm said.

"You won't," Felix assured her. "Here, put this on," he instructed Storm and handed her the prettiest cat collar she had ever seen. It was lilac velvet, her favourite colour and was covered in the shiniest, brightest jewels she had ever seen.

"Greedy Fat Cat and his ratty crew will not be able to resist it," Felix said, as he smiled at how well the collar suited Storm.

"Where did you get this, Felix?" Storm asked the young fox. "It's beautiful."

"It was my mother's. She gave it to me when she left home with my sisters," he told her.

"I can't let you risk losing something as valuable as this," Storm said, as she started to undo the collar.

"Just don't let them catch you," Felix said, reaching out with his paw to prevent her removing it. "That lazy, no good, bunch of villains needs all the incentives we can offer to get them to give chase. I need them all to leave their headquarters, and this might be the incentive that thieving lot will need."

Felix led the way towards a vantage point halfway up a fire escape on a building about fifty metres from the evil gang's hideout. "From here, you will be able to see where I go to meet with them. Keep watching the entrance I use, and when they come out to chase you, take off and run as fast as you can. From here you will have fifty metres head start, which hopefully will be close enough for them to think they can catch you but far enough away that you don't get caught. It's up to you whether you take the quicker, rooftop route or the safer but much longer, street level escape route," Felix explained.

"I want to go via the rooftops," Storm declared nervously.

"Are you sure?" Felix asked. Storm nodded her head, but the truth was, she'd never been as unsure about something as she was then.

"Good, that will slow them down," Felix encouraged her. "Just keep looking forward and mind the gap between some of the buildings. The route I've given you doesn't have many, but unfortunately there are some. Nothing a cat can't cope with," Felix explained.

That would be any normal cat, no doubt, Storm pointed out to herself.

"Solo and I will see you at Paddington," Felix said, reassuringly. "Good luck!"

Storm watched Felix cross the deserted street, heading towards Greedy Fat Cat's HQ. He turned to check if she could see where he was going and to be certain that Storm, and more importantly the valuable collar around her neck, could be clearly seen in the dim light. Then, Felix disappeared into the gang's lair.

"Ah, good morning," Greedy Fat Cat called out, when Felix appeared through the door. "What have you got us for breakfast? More than you brought yesterday, I hope?" the evil boss asked menacingly.

"Did I hear someone say breakfast?" asked the big-boned rat as he woke from his slumber.

"I haven't got you any food yet; I was on my way when something distracted me that I think you will be interested in," Felix tempted Greedy Fat Cat.

"Do tell?" the villain encouraged the fox.

"There's a lost cat across the street. By the look of things, she has some very rich owners, judging by the diamond studded collar around her neck," Felix said.

"Diamonds?" the Greedy Fat Cat couldn't resist clarifying.

"Yes, lots of them and big ones too," the young fox confirmed.

Just as Felix had expected, without hesitation, the Greedy Fat Cat took the bait. "Come on, boys, we have work to do!" he ordered his motley crew. Unable to resist the temptation of rich pickings, the rodents and their evil boss took off in pursuit of their next vulnerable victim.

***

Storm had not taken her eyes off the doorway Felix had disappeared through just a few minutes earlier. "There she is!" she heard the ring-leader rat shout, as he pointed towards Storm from across the street.

"Get her!" Greedy Fat Cat shrieked, as the rodent trio began running towards her. Quickly, Storm bounded up the fire escape, two stairs at a time, up onto the rooftop above.

Where do I go now? she asked herself as the fear of being caught by her pursuers overwhelmed Storm. It erased from her mind the details of the escape routes which she had so diligently committed to memory. She had no choice but to hope her feline instincts would serve her well.

***

"Solo?" Storm's mother heard someone whisper from somewhere in the darkness that constantly surrounded her. She stopped purring and opened her eyes, which unfortunately did nothing to enlighten her as to where the voice had come from or indeed who the voice belonged to. "Solo?" the unfamiliar voice asked again, closer to her this time. She didn't recognise the voice, but she was certain it wasn't one of her evil captors; it sounded too warm and friendly for that.

"Yes?" Solo replied.

"My name is Felix. I am a friend of your daughter," the voice informed her, as she heard the key beginning to turn in her prison cell door. Quickly, Solo instinctively threw herself against the door in a futile attempt to prevent the stranger from entering the guest room. Solo would have been no match for the fox if he'd chosen to push against her, but he didn't, instead he waited.

Patiently, hoping that Solo would allow him to convince her that he was there to help.

"You say you are a friend of my daughter?" Solo asked for clarification.

"Yes, I am a friend of your daughter," Felix said.

"Forgive me if that doesn't convince me I should trust you, considering what happened to me the last time someone told me they were a friend of my daughter. How do I know I can trust you?" Solo enquired, standing firm with her back pressed hard against the door.

Felix had to admit, she did have a point. Pretending to be her daughter's friend sounded like the sneaky type of approach her evil kidnappers might have taken. "Her name is Storm...," he said. Solo said nothing in reply. She remained silent, giving nothing away. Clearly simply knowing Storm's name wasn't enough to convince her he was there to help. "And I'm very sorry about what happened to Casper," Felix quickly added.

"Storm told you about Casper?" Solo asked. "She never talks about Casper to anyone," she challenged him.

"Perhaps that meant she considered me her friend," the shrewd fox suggested.

"What did she tell you about Casper?" Solo pressed.

"That he was a beautiful white cat, and his eyes were different colours," he said. "You must have been very proud of him."

"Yes, I was, and I still am," Solo admitted as she stepped aside to allow Felix to open the door.

"We need to be quick in case those villains come back. I'm here to take you to Storm," Felix said, appalled by the bleak and squalid conditions Storm's mother had been forced to endure at the hands of Greedy Fat Cat.

"Are you able to follow me?" he asked.

"As long as I can hear where you are, then I can follow you," Solo offered. "Do you whistle?" she asked.

"Not this early in the morning, I don't; can you hand me your collar?" Felix asked. "I notice you have a bell on it, perhaps you could follow the sound of that... if I can fit it round my neck," he said, realising how small it looked.

"What are you?" Solo asked, suddenly remembering what her daughter had said about asking strangers that question more often.

"I'm a fox," Felix said, as he took the collar from Solo.

"A fox. What do you look like?" she asked.

"Like a fox." Felix couldn't resist joking. "I'm sorry," he quickly said, realising that Solo may never have seen a fox before. "Well, my fur is coloured red with some white bits, and I also have a very bushy tail and a wider neck than a cat," he explained as he lengthened Solo's collar as far as it would go.

"I thought you might be a fox; I recognised the smell," Solo said. "We have foxes where we live but I don't have much to do with them. I think they're wary of me, perhaps because I'm blind," she told the young fox.

"Well, more fool them; it's their loss," Felix said, choking as he fastened Solo's little collar around his neck.

"I didn't mean to suggest that you smell," Solo said. "It's just that I have a very keen sense of smell because of my blindness."

"That's okay, you don't have to apologise; I know foxes smell. It's how we keep intruders off our territories," Felix replied. "Right, let's go before I pass out with this tight collar round my neck," he instructed Solo, as the bell tinkled with every step he took. Felix led the way out of the villains' lair and headed for their rendezvous point with Storm at Paddington Station. With the first part of his plan complete, the young fox hoped desperately that Solo's daughter would remember the way and manage to stay out of the clutches of Greedy Fat Cat and his evil gang.

***

Storm had no choice but to follow her instincts as a result of having forgotten her escape route. She had remembered noticing on Felix's map that as long as she kept the river behind her then she would be sure she was heading north towards Paddington. That was all she could remember, though, apart from Felix warning her to 'Mind the Gap' but she couldn't recall what he meant by that. Storm had already covered a significant distance over the many rooftops she had crossed, however, her pursuers were still much closer than she would have liked.

"There she is!" the ring-leader rat shouted from the rooftop behind her, encouraging his boss to pick up the pace. "We're catching up with her."

"Where's she heading?" Greedy Fat Cat asked when he reached the ring-leader rat, hoping it would buy him enough time to catch his breath.

"I'm not sure," the ring-leader rat said. "She's probably lost; you know how stupid the rich are, more money than sense."

Greedy Fat Cat wasn't sure how to take that, considering how wealthy he was as a result of his criminal activities. He'd always believed it was the poor who were stupid.

Storm wasn't rich, but she was lost, and she had run out of rooftops. As she quickly surveyed the horizon, she hoped to catch sight of Paddington Station or at least something that resembled a railway station. She noted the river was indeed a long way behind her, so she had at least been heading in the right direction. However, her pursuers were not that far behind and closing in fast. *Where now?* Storm asked herself, not for the first time.

Either side of her, there were no adjoining rooftops and the closest rooftop ahead looked too far away. *I can't possibly jump such a distance, so high off the ground*, she convinced herself as her fear of heights returned. Hearing her pursuers getting closer only served to overwhelm her. The evil villains were no more than one rooftop behind her and showing no signs of giving up the chase any time soon.

Carefully, Storm edged her way to the brink of the huge gap between the two buildings. *This must be the gap that Felix had warned me about*, she thought, as she peered over the edge of the roof down to the street below and began to tremble. She hated heights; *How have I been stupid enough to let Felix talk me into this? How did I think I could carry out this ridiculous stunt, and why couldn't Mum just stay on the bouncy castle?* were just some of the thoughts racing through her mind.

Then she heard a cry, "Storm!" It was Felix shouting up to her from across the alleyway below. "Don't look down, just keep looking ahead. You're nearly there," he

encouraged her. Storm could hear the chasing gang getting closer.

"I can't do this," she called back to Felix.

"Yes, you can," the young fox argued. "I have Solo with me, and she's fine. You have to do this, Storm, for all our sakes. Please?" Felix pleaded.

"Storm, it's your mother," Solo shouted up to her. "Please trust us, you can do this," she begged her daughter.

"I don't know how to," Storm cried back.

"Close your eyes, and trust your feline instincts," her mother encouraged her.

"You're cornered, my dear; you have nowhere to go!" Storm heard Greedy Fat Cat shout from behind her. The evil gang were now on the same roof as her.

"Keep your eyes closed and think of Casper!" she heard her mother shout. "It's what I do." Storm couldn't help but remember the last time her mother attempted to jump somewhere; it wasn't that successful as she recalled… but at least her mother had tried.

Is this it? Storm asked herself. *Is this the limit to what I can achieve?* For years she'd regretted not having the opportunity to save her twin brother, yet now that she had a chance to save herself and her mother, she couldn't do it.

Slowly, Storm closed her eyes, and suddenly an image of Casper appeared before her. She couldn't help but smile at his mischievous grin.

"You can do this, sis!" she heard him say. "It's a piece of cake!" A tear trickled down her face as she recalled how he used to say that all the time when they were kittens. Storm crouched down on her haunches, ready to pounce, just like she did when she and Casper used to play fight in the garden. Keeping her eyes tightly shut and driven by the image of Casper vividly in her mind, she launched herself with all her might, out over the edge of the high building and across the alleyway that lay many floors below her.

Chapter 8
Tunnel Vision

Storm didn't consider herself athletic; she would argue that she was more apathetic than athletic, indifferent towards anything resembling exertion or exercise. But fortunately, her feline instincts served her well as she flew between the two buildings with the grace and agility expected of an overweight warthog. SMACK! Storm landed clumsily on the adjacent roof.

"Follow her!" Storm heard Greedy Fat Cat shout to the three rats who nervously peered down at her from the rooftop above.

"With all due respect, Boss, aren't cats better at jumping than rats?" the ring-leader rat asked.

"Any self-respecting cat of my standing would never dream of jumping across there. You get her!" Greedy Fat Cat ordered as he joined his rodent gang looking down at Storm from the rooftop above her.

Storm slowly got to her feet; dazed and in shock at what she had just done, she gradually resumed her escape. Storm thought she recalled hearing her mother and Felix calling up to her from the street below, but she wasn't sure. Having hit her head hard when she clattered onto the rooftop, Storm wasn't sure of anything anymore, except that she had to get off the roof and closer to ground level. Spotting a fire escape, she made her way down it.

"Quick, she's getting away! Let's go down the fire escape on this building and cut her off in the street!" Greedy Fat Cat screamed.

It was a race between Storm and her pursuers to see who would reach the street first. Storm was dizzy and disorientated; she had fallen heavier than she would have liked. The dazed cat made her way gingerly down the fire escape. She was well aware of the need to do it quickly, but the chase and her fall were taking their toll on her.

"In here!" Felix called to Storm through a window next to her when she was halfway down the fire escape.

"Felix!" Storm cried, "They are coming; they mustn't see you. Run!"

"Don't worry about them," Felix said. "I know a secret way to the station." Carefully he helped Storm clamber through the half-open window. "Your mother is waiting for us at the back of this building. From there, it's just a short distance to Paddington. Do you think you can make it?" he asked.

"I think so," she replied.

With the stealth of a fox, Felix led the way through a series of dimly lit rooms and corridors. They emerged into the stark daylight of the bright winter's day at the back of the building. Morning had just broken, and with it came another clear blue sky and blinding winter sunlight.

"Storm?" her mother asked as Storm's eyes struggled with the sudden transition from the darkness of the building to the bright daylight.

"Mum?" Storm asked, not sure where her mother was.

"Are you okay?" Solo asked her.

"I think so," Storm replied, hesitantly. Felix couldn't help but smile seeing the two cats talking to one another but not really facing the right way due to their respective temporary and permanent blindness.

"We need to get going," Felix said.

"But I've made some good money here," Solo said.

"What?" Felix asked.

"Begging, here. I've got some money, look!" Solo said, proudly pointing to the floor where a few pound coins and even a five-pound note lay. She'd only been stood in the street for a few minutes, but it appeared the people of Paddington were every bit as generous as the people in Grosvenor Square.

"Good," Felix said, not really sure what the correct response should be. "Well, we'd better collect your takings then… and get going, before Greedy Fat Cat gets here," he suggested.

The trio made their way across the street and down a back alley towards Paddington Station. Felix led them to a small door at the rear of the station and held it open to allow Storm and her mother to make their way through it.

"There's another door in front of you, which is a maintenance door that leads through to the freight railway line that only runs during the night. There should be no trains running there during the day," Felix said as he closed the door behind him.

"And...?" Storm asked.

"And," Felix said, "the railway track runs from London to the gravel pits west of the city. From what your mother told me earlier, I suspect that's close to where you live. You can follow the track almost all the way home," he told them, proud of how much he knew about the comings and goings of his home, London town.

"Where will you go, Felix?" Storm asked, with a tone of concern.

"I'll go back home. I need to make sure no one steals my territory," the young fox said, as if it were an obvious thing to do. "Just keep to the tracks, and you'll be fine; hopefully, you'll eventually see something that you recognise near to where you live. With any luck, your home will be there, waiting for you," he smiled, hoping it would give them the encouragement it looked as if they needed.

"Thank you, Felix," Storm said solemnly, not really knowing what else to say.

"It's no problem; I just hope you find your home. Good luck," Felix said, before he turned to leave them.

"What do we do now?" Solo asked, when she heard the door close behind Felix.

"I guess we should start walking," her daughter replied, "but you'll need to turn around first, Mum. You're facing the wrong way," Storm explained politely to her mother.

Storm couldn't see a thing when she opened the maintenance door that led through to the railway line. "I don't like the look of this," she said, standing in the doorway.

"Why not?" her mother asked.

"I can't see anything; its pitch black in there," Storm explained.

"Welcome to my world," Solo said.

Storm remained silent, acknowledging what her mother had just said. She had never really appreciated how difficult it must be for her mother to be in constant darkness. Storm hated the dark, even more than she hated heights.

"There's nothing to be frightened of," her mother said reassuringly. "If I can cope with darkness, anyone can; you just have to rely on your other senses a bit more. I'll lead the way if you like," Solo offered, recalling that she'd never said that to anyone before and probably wouldn't do ever again.

"Do you mind?" Storm asked.

"Of course not, I'm your mother," Solo said as she stepped through the doorway and was greeted by the stench of dampness and diesel oil on the railway track.

The tunnel seemed to go on forever in front of them, and Storm couldn't see the end of it. "How long

is this tunnel?" she asked as she followed closely behind her mother.

"Don't let the darkness make you anxious," Solo said. "Not all darkness is bad; darkness can be calming and can free you from distraction, giving you time to reflect. Don't forget, the brightest stars shine during the darkest of nights," she suggested to her daughter and then began to purr.

Solo's purring made it easier for Storm to follow her in the pitch darkness, and its rhythm was somewhat comforting to her. As they continued down the dark tunnel, Storm thought about her mother's blindness and how she hadn't appreciated just how difficult it must be for Solo. Simple tasks that Storm took for granted must be so much more difficult when you can't even see your paw in front of you. *How does Mum remain so content with life?* Storm wondered. *I can't remember Mum ever complaining about anything.* She felt ashamed; Storm wished she had not blamed her mother for what happened to Casper, *but then who else could I have blamed? I had to blame someone.* She wondered how Solo could forgive anyone for blaming her and for being so intolerant of her blindness. Perhaps her mother's catzheimers had indeed rendered her crazy. Storm was at least relieved about not abandoning Solo in London; she had to confess to considering it but admitted, *without Mum, I would not be coping with this tunnel.*

"It was nice of Felix to help us," Solo said, disturbing the silence between them.

"Yes, it was," Storm replied, surprising her mother who never expected a reply from her.

"Where did you meet him?" Solo asked.

"I'm not sure; I was lost, and he found me," Storm recalled.

"He seems more feline than canine to me, don't you think?" Solo asked.

"Yes, I do," Storm agreed, recalling how struck she was by the likeness. "I hope he gets home safely; those villains are nasty."

"Rats usually are... and they smell a lot," Solo said.

"How did you notice Felix had feline characteristics?" Storm asked.

"How he walked; his footsteps were light and not at all clumsy like Bracken," Solo explained, "and he sprays his territory."

"How do you know that?!" Storm asked.

"Oh, he told me," Solo said. Storm smiled; only her mother was capable of discussing something as sensitive as 'spraying' with someone she'd only just met.

Suddenly, Solo stopped walking causing Storm to walk into her, just like Solo had walked into Storm so many times before. "Sorry!" Storm said apologetically.

"Did you hear that?" her mother asked.

"No, what?" Storm asked.

"Shhh, I think I heard something," her mother said.

"Gotcha!" yelled Greedy Fat Cat. He and his rodent gang suddenly appeared in front of Solo and Storm, shining a bright torch in their faces.

"Where do you think you two are going?" he asked menacingly.

"Home," Solo replied defiantly.

"You can't go home," Greedy Fat Cat said. "You have work to do, and you, my dear..." he continued, turning to shine his torch at Storm, "have something I want."

"Get away from us, you... you... you evil monster!" Storm shouted.

"Oh, a feisty cat," Greedy Fat Cat chuckled. "I can assure you I've been called much worse than that, my dear. You have something I want. In fact, you have two things I want: your stupid blind mother and that collar you're wearing. Now give it to me before I set my rats on you."

"We're not afraid of your rats, or you!" Solo shouted.

"You should be!" the ring-leader rat said. He stepped in front of Solo and held something sharp against her throat and said, "You have some begging to do for us!"

"Give me that collar," Greedy Fat Cat said again to Storm, "or the old cat gets it."

"Don't give it to them," Solo said firmly.

"Can't you see she's blind?" Storm asked.

"What do I care?" Greedy Fat Cat asked. "Blind or not blind, she can still beg."

"You're an evil, horrid cat," Storm said as she reluctantly began removing the diamond collar from her neck.

"Don't give it to him!" Solo shouted again.

"I have no choice, Mum; they'll take it anyway," Storm said resignedly as she handed the collar to Greedy Fat Cat.

"Good girl," Greedy Fat Cat said. "Now, I wonder how much your owners would pay in ransom money for your safe return," he mused.

"You've got what you wanted, now leave us alone," Storm pleaded. Suddenly there was an ear-splitting howl that echoed down the tunnel and engulfed them all.

"What on earth was that?" shrieked the thin rat holding his hands over his large ears.

"HOOOWWWL," the sound rang out again only closer to them this time.

"I think we should go, Boss!" the big-boned rat suggested.

Without warning, Felix appeared and threw himself at Greedy Fat Cat, spitting and hissing as he pinned the no-good villain to the floor. "Let them go!" the fox screeched in a voice that no-one would have associated with the young fox. It was clear he was angry, very angry. The young fox stood on Greedy Fat Cat's chest holding him to the floor, awaiting his response.

"You shouldn't do this, Felix," Greedy Fat Cat said sheepishly, clearly intimidated by the young fox's aggression.

"I mean it!" Felix said, sensing the crook doubting his intentions. "LET THEM GO!" the angry fox howled.

Greedy Fat Cat said nothing, he just nodded in submission. Felix stepped off Greedy Fat Cat allowing him to stand up. Without a word, Greedy Fat Cat brushed his knotted fur as if it would help him regain his dignity and nodded to his rodent crew beckoning them away from Solo and Storm. Once the motley crew were a safe distance away from Felix, Greedy Fat Cat shouted, "You'll regret this, Felix. Just you wait!"

"Shall we go?" Felix asked Solo and Storm, choosing to ignore the threats coming from Greedy Fat Cat.

"But what about your territory, Felix?" Storm asked.

"I don't think I will have one now judging by how upset Greedy Fat Cat is. No doubt, The Exterminator will be on his way there soon," the young fox surmised. "I'll walk with you at least until you get to the end of this tunnel," Felix said.

"Thank you," Storm said, "for saving us again."

"You're welcome," Felix said, winking at Storm as he did so. Not that Storm could see him in the pitch darkness which engulfed them again now that Greedy Fat Cat and his torch had gone.

"Here's your collar back," Storm said. "I suspect that's why you came after us."

"No, it isn't. Actually, I was worried that lot might find you. Besides, I had to give Solo her collar back; it's killing me, and it's far too noisy," the young fox explained as he handed Solo's collar back to her.

"Well, here's your collar back anyway," Storm insisted.

"You wear it for now, I've got nowhere to put it," Felix said.

The three of them resumed their journey into the darkness. They were led by Solo and the sound of the tinkling bell on her collar, which echoed back at them from the tunnel walls that surrounded them.

"Does she always purr?" Felix whispered to Storm.

"Only when she's not talking," Storm told him.

"So basically, she always makes a noise of some sort?" Felix asked.

"Yes, I suppose she does," Storm replied. "I hadn't thought of it like that."

"Are we nearly there yet?" Solo asked, interrupting their whispered conversation.

"No, not yet," Felix said. "Soon."

Sure enough, the fox was true to his word, and a small dot of light growing before them began to herald the end of the tunnel. Instinctively, the three of them picked up their pace, heading towards the beckoning daylight. As they exited the tunnel, both Storm and Felix struggled to see anything as their eyes were blinded by the bright daylight. Solo, on the other hand, experienced no difficulty in adjusting; she welcomed the sensation of sunlight on her back.

"I can't see a thing," Storm cried.

"Me neither," Felix said, as he rubbed his eyes with his front paws.

"Feel that sunlight," Solo said as she sat on the railway track and stared straight at the blinding sun above them.

They all sat on the railway track for a while enjoying what little heat there was in the winter sunshine and relishing the crisp fresh air after their time in the dirty, damp, diesel-soaked railway tunnel.

Chapter 9
Lost and Found!

Once Felix's eyes had adjusted to the daylight he asked, "Can you see any signposts indicating how much further it is?"

"Sign posts?" Storm asked. "We're not in the city now; we're in the countryside. There are no signposts telling you where to go here, except on the roads."

"Oh, I see," Felix said. He realised he had never ventured much beyond his territory, let alone gone as far out of the city as they appeared to be. "How do you know where to go then?" the young fox asked. "Doesn't everyone get lost?"

"Sometimes," Solo said, "but then you normally ask someone for directions, anyone."

"You mean, you might ask a complete stranger?" Felix enquired, stunned at the idea of even speaking to a complete stranger, let alone asking them to tell you where to go. Life in the city seldom required anyone to speak to a complete stranger; in fact, in many territories it was even considered rude. In London, there were always discarded street maps left by the tourists or signs pointing you in the direction you needed to go and also signs telling you where you shouldn't go. If they didn't work, you could always ask a policeman but never a complete stranger.

"You spoke to me," Storm pointed out to Felix.

"That was different; you were lost, and I wasn't," Felix explained.

"What difference does that make?" Storm asked.

Felix said nothing. Storm had a point; he had spoken to her, and they were indeed strangers. He hadn't thought of it like that. He just considered it was his job to know everyone who ventured onto his territory.

"But I'm glad you did speak to me," Storm said as she smiled at Felix. "Should we just keep following the tracks?" she asked.

Felix stood up and stared at the rail track ahead of them. "We could but the line splits into two a few metres ahead. Do you know which one you should take?" he asked.

"No. So we're lost then," Storm said. "We'll need to ask someone."

"Who can we ask? It's not exactly crowded here; in fact, it looks deserted to me," Felix said, looking around. "Do you know where Solo is?" he asked when he noticed she wasn't there.

"Oh wonderful! So, not only are we lost, now I've lost my mother again," Storm concluded.

"She couldn't have gone far," Felix told her as he looked around at the thick undergrowth covering the railway embankments on either side of the track.

"You don't know her, Felix. Trust me, she could be anywhere by now," Storm said hopelessly.

"Shhh, listen. Can you hear that?" Felix asked. In the distance, he heard the soft tinkling of a bell.

***

"Hello, is there anyone there?" Solo asked as she stopped dead in her tracks having heard something rustling in the undergrowth close by. There was no reply. "We're lost, can you help us please?" Solo persisted. Then, there was movement, and a voice spoke out.

"Where do you want to go?" the stranger asked.

"We're trying to get home," Solo said.

"Where is your home?" the stranger enquired.

"I'm not sure. I know where it should be, but it drifted away with the floods. We are hoping it will be back where it should be by now," Solo explained.

"Who are 'we'?" the stranger asked, sounding much closer to her this time, which made Solo flinch. Even her acute sense of hearing hadn't picked up the sound of the stranger stealthily moving toward her through the undergrowth.

"Me… and my daughter," replied Solo.

"Where is your daughter?" the stranger asked from behind Solo now.

"B-b-back by the tunnel," Solo stuttered nervously.

"Why should I help two cats?" the stranger asked. "Cats kill things for fun," the voice said menacingly.

***

"I can't hear anything," Storm told Felix.

"I thought I heard Solo's bell, but now I can't hear anything either," Felix explained. "She must have stopped moving."

"Mu-" Storm began to call out before Felix stopped her, putting his paw across her mouth.

"Shhh, don't shout. We don't know where we are. This could be someone's territory, and we could be trespassing." The wily fox advised Storm, "Hopefully your mother will move again soon, and we will be able to track her down."

"If she's not dead already," Storm muttered, clearly anxious. It had not occurred to her they might be on someone else's territory.

***

"I've never killed anything in my life," Solo insisted to the stranger. "I'm blind; how could I catch anything?"

"With great difficulty, I suspect," the stranger said, less menacingly now. Clearly the stranger had let down their guard, much to Solo's relief. "I'm sorry if I scared you," the stranger said, "but I don't like animals that kill things for pleasure. Plus, you are on my territory."

"I'm sorry if we're trespassing; we just followed the railway track," Solo explained.

"You know the track splits into two here," the stranger pointed out.

"No, I didn't," Solo confessed.

"From what you say about the floods, I would suggest you take the left-hand track. That should lead you to the gravel pits; from there, your daughter should at least recognise her surroundings, unless of course she's also blind," the stranger said.

"She's not blind yet, thank goodness," Solo said subdued.

The stranger felt sorry for her and wished there was something they could say to reassure Solo, but the stranger had heard of parents passing on their blindness to their children.

"Thank you for the directions," Solo said, changing the subject of their discussion. "My daughter and I will leave your territory right away. I'm sorry for trespassing," Solo smiled in the general direction of the stranger.

"I hope you find your home," the stranger said as Solo retreated back through the undergrowth towards the tunnel and her companions.

***

"Listen, she's on the move!" Felix said on hearing Solo's bell tinkle again.

"Where have you been?" Storm asked her mother when she emerged through the undergrowth. "We've been worried sick," she chastised her mother.

"Getting directions," Solo told her, as if it should be obvious where she'd been.

"You could have been killed out there! Had it ever occurred to you we might be trespassing on someone else's territory?" Storm asked.

"Of course, it had. That's why I went to get directions. I presumed if this was a territory, then there must be someone here who knew the place well and could give us directions," her mother explained.

"And?" Storm asked, disguising her embarrassment at being the only one who hadn't realised they might be on someone's territory.

"And what?" Solo replied.

"And, did you get directions?" her daughter asked with exasperation, still angry at her mother recklessly wandering off in a strange place.

"Apparently, the railway track splits into two here," Solo announced proudly.

"Yes, we already know that," Storm snapped.

"Well, we need to take the left-hand one," Solo told them.

"How do you know?" Felix asked, joining in on the conversation.

"A stranger told me, apparently we're on their territory," Solo enlightened him.

"What kind of stranger?" Felix asked.

"I don't know," Solo confessed, "I didn't ask but judging by the smell, I'd say it was a…"

"Felix?" a voice asked. The stranger Solo had spoken to stepped out from the undergrowth beside them.

"Mum?" Felix quizzed.

Felix hardly recognised his mother. Her fur was greyer than he remembered' and she had lost weight, too. Clearly, life in the country wasn't as easy as he'd imagined.

"You've grown a lot," his mother said as she touched noses with Felix. She was crying, and if the young fox had not had his travelling companions with him, he would have cried too. It had been a long time in the young fox's life since he'd last seen his mother. How he had missed her and his sisters.

"Are my sisters still with you?" Felix asked, holding back the tears.

"Yes, they are," his mother said. "We have a big territory here, and I'm getting too old to manage it. Your sisters do most of the patrolling, but they should be starting their own families, not stuck here looking

after their old mum. What about you, Felix, do you have a family?" she asked.

"Yes, you and my sisters," Felix said proudly.

"No, I meant your own family, in London?" his mother pressed.

"No, I don't," Felix said sadly. "There are not many vixens around, and anyway, the city is no place to bring up a young family. You said so yourself before you all left."

"That isn't why we left, Felix," his mother said. "Your sisters and I had to leave."

"What do you mean 'had to'?" Felix enquired.

"Greedy Fat Cat forced us to go; he didn't like vixens being around. He said we would distract the male foxes who were working for him, which was bad for business. He threatened that if I didn't leave and take your sisters with me, he would send in the Dockland rats."

"And The Exterminators would come and kill us all?" Felix interjected.

"That's right, how did you know?" his mother asked.

"Just a lucky guess," Felix said.

"I couldn't expose our family to that risk, so that's why we left the city. It broke my heart leaving you and our home, but what else could I do? I'm so sorry, Felix, we've all missed you so much."

"You don't have to apologise, Mum, I understand. You won't be pleased to hear that Greedy Fat Cat is still using the same threat to get his own way. That's why I am here with Solo and Storm," Felix said pointing to each of his companions.

"I'm sorry if I frightened you, Solo," Felix's mother said.

"Don't worry, I'm used to it," Solo assured her.

"That collar looks good on you, Storm," his mother said, turning towards her. Storm had forgotten she still wore the collar. She touched it with her paw as if trying to disguise the fact she was wearing the expensive gift Felix's mother had given to him.

"You're a long way from your territory, Felix," his mother said, searching for an explanation as to why her son was here with his unusual travelling companions.

"I don't think I will have a territory now. My guess is that, after what I did to him, Greedy Fat Cat will have already called in the rats," Felix informed his mother.

"Where will you go?" his mother asked.

"I'm not sure. I promised Solo and Storm I would stay with them this far, but now I guess we should part company," Felix said, sad at the prospect of leaving his friends.

"Stay here with us," his mother suggested. "Your sisters would love to see you again." The young fox was hesitant about leaving Solo and Storm.

"Don't worry about us," Solo spoke out having sensed the young fox's hesitation.

"Are you sure?" Felix asked.

"Of course, now go and be with your family. Oh, and don't forget your mum's collar," Storm said, reaching to remove the beautiful collar from around her neck.

"Keep it," Felix's mum insisted. "It suits you. Besides, I have everything I need now. My family is together again, thanks to you two. Once you've found your home, you should come and visit us now that you know where we live."

"We'd like that very much," Storm said.

Felix sat with his mother and watched the two cats make their way down the railway track in search of their lost home. Felix was pleased his mother had insisted that Storm kept the collar, but he was worried she and Solo might not find their home and wouldn't be reunited again with their family like he had been. He desperately hoped they would.

"Was it left, or right?" he heard Solo asking her daughter as they reached the junction in the railway track. Storm said nothing she just carried on up the left-hand track.

"Left then," Solo said as she followed her daughter down the track.

Felix smiled at the odd couple disappearing down the track; they were the only friends he'd ever had who had given him so much amusement. He wondered if there was anything about her mother that didn't annoy Storm. The young fox was already missing them both and was sad to think he might not see them again. Foxes weren't meant to like animals that killed things for fun, his mother had always told him. Felix knew some cats did that, but he couldn't imagine Solo or Storm ever had.

Chapter 10
The Purrfect Mother!

"His mother seemed very nice!" Solo said, taking a break from purring after what she thought was a more than long enough period of silence between her and her daughter. Storm said nothing, she just kept walking. "I mean, letting you keep that collar was a really nice thing to do, and she gave us directions home." Still there was no response from her daughter. Solo's fine hearing picked up a sniffle. She wondered if Storm was crying because Felix had gone. She decided to change the subject. "You know, his mother had me worried for a while when I first met her," Solo said. "She told me that she didn't like cats, because we kill things for fun. Have you ever killed anything?" she asked.

"Not yet... but there's always a first time," Storm replied, distracted from her grief for a moment.

Solo was relieved, things were getting back to normal between them, and soon they would be home and back with Bracken. Solo began to purr, as she always did when she wasn't talking. "Do you ever not make a noise?" Storm asked her as they continued on their way.

"Not really," her mother replied before resuming her purring, even louder as if to emphasise the point.

"What have you missed the most?" Solo asked.

"What?" Storm replied.

"When we get home, what will you be most pleased to see?" her mother repeated.

Storm shook her head and sighed, knowing there was more to come.

"I think I'll be most pleased to see Bracken," Solo said. "But then, Grant does make sure we always have food and water, so it might be him. But then Alison is so kind, and she regularly brushes us, so it might be her," Solo continued. "Or maybe... it won't be any of them. Maybe I'll be most pleased to see my bed again, or Alison's garden... or mayb—"

"For goodness sake, Mum, are you going to babble on all the way home?" Storm asked, stopping so quickly that her mother walked into her. "Who cares who you will be most pleased to see, I will just be pleased to be home. I don't have favourites," Storm explained. Solo kept quiet; over the years she'd learned to recognise when it was fun to goad her daughter or not.

"Sorry," Solo said sheepishly, then returned to her habitual purring.

They had been walking a while down the railway track when Storm turned a sweeping bend, and there in front of them, lay a long expanse of water. It was a flooded gravel pit quarry. Fortunately, this time Solo managed to avoid walking into the back of her daughter when she stopped abruptly.

"Why have you stopped?" Solo asked. "Are we there?"

"No, but we've reached the quarry," her daughter replied.

"That's good, isn't it?" her mother enquired.

"It would be, if the quarry wasn't full of water," Storm moaned. Solo didn't know what to say; disadvantaged by being unable to see their surroundings, it was difficult for her to immediately suggest a solution.

"Can we go around it?" she asked, when Storm hadn't offered anything.

"Judging by how long the quarry looks, that would take days. Are you up to that?" Storm asked, turning to look at her aging mother.

"Probably not," Solo conceded after only a little hesitation.

"The quarry's not very wide though," Storm said with what her mother hoped was an air of positivity. Solo's optimism was cut short when Storm added, "But the water looks very deep."

Both Solo and Storm sat quietly at the edge of the quarry contemplating their next move. Getting colder and increasingly hungry, Solo asked, "Can we jump over it?"

"What, with your jumping track record?" her daughter asked rather scathingly, her anxiety levels steadily rising.

"Sorry for holding you back. I just can't walk much further," Solo said apologetically. Storm said nothing;

they both returned to sitting in uncomfortable silence, made even more uncomfortable because Solo hadn't even resumed her purring.

"It's not you that's holding me back," Storm eventually confessed.

"What do you mean?" Solo asked, surprised to hear her daughter's revelation.

"It's me," Storm replied, turning to face her mother. "It's my fear of heights," she further revealed.

"I thought it was water that was stopping us. What's that got to do with you not liking heights?" Solo asked with more than a hint of maternal sympathy in her voice.

"There is another way to get across the water, instead of walking all the way around it," Storm explained.

"How?" Solo asked.

"There's some kind of mining equipment that spans the quarry from one side to the other but it's very narrow... and extremely high," Storm said, looking up towards a rusting mining conveyor belt. It pointed up into the sky on the opposite side of the quarry, and then flattened out as it stretched across the quarry below it, before descending much too quickly for Storm's liking, towards the ground beside them on their side of the lake.

"Is it very high?" Solo asked sensing apprehension in her daughter's voice. "Don't be afraid, Storm, we can

do this," Solo said with as much enthusiasm as she could muster with her empty stomach and tired legs. "I'll lead the way, and you just have to follow me."

"Mum, are you forgetting you're blind, and I'm really scared of heights? How on earth can we climb that?" Storm challenged her.

"Trust me, Storm. Have I ever let you down?" her mother asked.

Had Storm not been as frightened as she was of heights and her mother's navigational skills, she would have laughed at Solo's unwavering optimism.

"If you are afraid of heights," Solo began, "you need to approach this like I do."

This'll be good, Storm thought to herself.

"Close your eyes…," Solo instructed her. "Are they closed?"

"Yes," Storm replied, keeping one of them open, so she could keep an eye on what her mother was up to.

"I didn't hear both eyelids closing," Solo said, astounding Storm with her acute sense of hearing. Storm closed her other eye, reluctantly.

"Good, now try and imagine this; you're safely back home dozing on the rug in front of the roaring log fire. Can you see that?" Solo asked.

"Yes, I can," Storm replied.

"Good, now keeping your eyes tightly closed, describe to me what you can hear," her mother instructed.

Storm thought about her homely surroundings and imagined the familiar activities that were going on and the sounds they made. "I can hear the log fire crackling beside me, and I can hear Alison's radio in the kitchen. Alison is preparing dinner for Grant and herself. I can hear the pots and pans clanging on the stove. I hear Bracken chewing his annoying, squeaky toy in his bed. I hear Grant moaning about something again, and I can hear the bell tinkling on your collar, and you bumping into things," Storm smiled to herself at the comforting images in her mind. "And I can hear the wind and rain hammering against the windows. Oh, and I can hear the cat flap rattling in the back door."

"That's brilliant!" she heard Solo shout from quite some distance. Storm's eyes snapped open to see where her mother was.

"I'm up here!" Solo cried. Storm looked towards the sky in disbelief and saw her mother perched at the very top of the mining conveyor belt.

"You'll have to come and help me!" her mother called down.

This could well be the most crazy, irresponsible and downright stupidest thing Mum has ever done, Storm thought to herself, furious at having been tricked by Solo.

"I can't come up there," Storm screamed at her mother.

"Yes, you can. You're a cat, and a good one at that," Solo encouraged her. Solo was taking a risk, but she figured she knew Storm would have no choice but to follow her up the narrow conveyor belt. Storm said nothing, Solo wondered if she'd misjudged her daughter and perhaps didn't know her at all. Her daughter's continued silence began to worry her.

Eventually Storm spoke. "Can you keep talking to me?" she shouted from where Solo sensed was at the bottom of the steep conveyor belt.

"Sure, what should I talk to you about?" Solo asked, not that she had ever asked Storm that question before.

"Tell me what you think Felix's mother is called?" Storm asked.

"Oh, I love guessing games! Let me see, I bet it's Martha. No, no, wait! I bet it's Felicity; no that's not a fox name. What about Simone? No, that won't be it either. I bet it's Joanne, or Deborah, or… it might be something more to do with nature, like Bracken!"

"No, that's a dog's name," her daughter answered from halfway up the mining conveyor belt. Solo smiled at how brave her daughter was being and continued talking. "Yes, of course it is. Well, what about Fern then? That's a good name for a fox. Yes, I like Fern, or maybe it's something like Autumn. That's like the colour of a fox, and it's to do with nature…"

"It's Amber," Storm said softly, right in front of Solo. She had successfully made it to the top! "His mother's name is Amber; he told me," Storm recalled.

"Well, that's a nice name," her mother said then. "Well done, Storm! You're so brave, and I would say, not scared of heights… one bit."

"We still have to cross over the water to the other side and then climb down," Storm informed her in a serious voice, emphasising that her ordeal was clearly far from over as far as she was concerned. Solo suspected Storm was extremely angry with her and that she probably would be in line for a serious telling off when they did reach the other side. *But it will be worth it*, she told herself, *at least we would be closer to home.*

Cautiously, Storm followed her mother along the narrow conveyor belt high above the freezing, cold water below. Storm held her head high and kept staring straight ahead, even though all she could see was Solo's rear end, her tail pointing straight up. Not a pretty sight, but it was better than looking down at the water far below. Slowly, they made their way across the conveyor belt. After what seemed an eternity to Storm, they reached the top of the conveyor belt that would take them back to the ground.

"I would never have guessed it was Amber," Solo said.

"You can stop talking now," Storm told her.

"Oh, okay, sorry," Solo replied and began purring instead. Solo made her way down the conveyor belt to the ground.

Solo braced herself for a royal scolding as she sat at the foot of the rusty structure, waiting for Storm to cautiously descend down the steep and narrow conveyor belt. Gingerly, her daughter made her way down towards Solo. "You tricked me," Storm accused Solo once her paws were safely back on solid ground.

"Sorry," Solo replied sheepishly, "but I knew you could do it."

"Thank you," Storm said, "for helping me. Now come on, let's get you home." She smiled and led the way.

Storm was secretly proud of herself for making it over the quarry, and now she was in familiar territory. They would be back where their home used to be in ten minutes or so; she just hoped their home would be there, along with the rest of her family. Solo followed her daughter closely, purring loudly, as the two weary travellers weaved their way down the streets that had been raging rivers only a few days before. Storm was worried that if Grant and Alison hadn't managed to drift back home by now, then they probably never would.

Storm stopped dead in her tracks, fighting back the tears at the wonderful sight before her. Although it was getting dark, Grant and Bracken were at the front of the house, messing about with something underneath it, and Alison was still picking up rubbish from the garden. Storm turned to face her mother. "We've made it," she told Solo and cried with relief. Our intrepid duo hugged each other, overwhelmed by what they had experienced during their adventure.

They had never spent as much time away from their home before, and neither had they spent as much time together, getting to know one another, for better and for worse.

Not surprisingly, Bracken was the first to notice Solo and Storm walking up the drive. Barking frantically, he ran to greet them. Solo braced herself for a barrage of innocent, but nevertheless, painful whacks on her head from his incessant tail-wagging. A few slaps of his tail would be nothing compared to what they'd both had to endure over the past few days. Solo was just delighted to be home and back with her family.

"Where have you two been?" Grant asked, not having even noticed they'd not been around if the truth was told.

"Alison, have you bought Storm a new collar?" Grant asked.

"No?" Alison replied.

"Thank goodness, because the one she has on looks very expensive," Grant said with relief.

After considerable head rubbing on both Grant and Alison's legs, Solo and Storm disappeared into the house. Exhausted and tired from their travels, they each made their way towards the safest, warmest and more importantly, the driest place they could think of to spend the night, Bracken's bed.

"You can have it," Solo said when she noticed her daughter had the same idea.

"It's big enough for the both of us," Storm pointed out, her warmth and willingness to share catching Solo by surprise. She smiled at the prospect of sleeping next to her daughter.

Solo nestled down close to Storm and made herself comfortable without too much circling, for fear of annoying her daughter.

"This…" Storm said softly once her mother had settled herself down.

"What?" Solo asked.

"You asked me what I had missed the most. It's this. Sleeping here with you," Storm replied.

Solo smiled and started to purr.

"Sorry, I'll stop purring," Solo apologised as soon as she realised what she was doing.

"Tell me, why do you purr all the time when you're not talking? I can understand why you might be doing it now, because you are happy to be home, but you purr even under the worst circumstances. Why?" Storm asked her mother.

"Since I lost my sight, I have always worried that one day the same thing might happen to you or Casper." Solo explained. "So, I promised myself that if either of you were ever to suddenly lose your sight, you would always know where to find me, because of my purring."

And with that, for the first time in her life, Storm began to see things more clearly. Because she had learned from her mother that 'seeing' is more than simply having the power of sight. It also requires an ability to understand and recognise the true value of life. Just as Solo always did.

~~~ THE END ~~~

Liked Seeing?

Don't miss Grant, Alison, and Bracken's adventure of what happened when the house floated away in:

Inspired by real-life events during flooding in a small leafy village on the banks of the River Thames just outside London. *Drifting* is an incredible story that should appeal to both children and adults alike. It follows the adventures of an ordinary couple who went to extraordinary lengths to protect their beautiful home.

Recent climate changes and the ever-increasing threat of flooding to us all makes our unlikely adventurers' story a truly relevant and enlightening experience. As we are taken on their journey of self-discovery and survival, we see friendships, both old and new, put to the test, as confidence and belief diminish with the challenges they encounter.

In a light-hearted manner, with illustrations, the story will inspire and educate children to recognise the true value of friendship and self-belief. As we see how important and rewarding it can be when we trust one another and never lose hope, no matter how bad things get. Reminding us that sometimes hope will be the only thing we have.